D1459315

- 5 AUG 2013

1 5 AUG 2016

- 2 SEP 2013

1 4 AUG 2019

2 4 JAN 2014

1 4 AUG 2019

BAS 11|19

1 2 SEP 2014

SHO 8/

1 0 JUL 2015

2 3 SEP 2015

1 3 APR 2016

WITHDRAWN FROM BROMLEY LIBRARIES

Bromley

THE LONDON BOROUGH
www.bromley.gov.uk

SHORTLANDS LIBRARY
020 8460 9692

Bromley

BETTER
the feel good place

Please return/renew this item
by the last date shown.
Books may also be renewed by
phone and Internet.

385.09

Bromley Libraries

3 0128 03060816 3

THE RED LAW

JACKSON GREGORY

SAGEBRUSH
Large Print Westerns

Copyright © 1941 by Jackson Gregory

First published in Great Britain by Hodder & Stoughton
First published in the United States by Dodd Mead

Published in Large Print 2012 by ISIS Publishing Ltd.,
7 Centremead, Osney Mead, Oxford OX2 0ES
by arrangement with
Golden West Literary Agency

BROMLEY
PUBLIC
LIBRARIES

AL

CLASS
WPB F

ACC
03060816

UI   30 NOV 2012

INVOICE DATE

All rights reserved

The moral right of the author has been asserted

British Library Cataloguing in Publication Data
Gregory, Jackson, 1882–1943.
   The red law.
   1. Western stories.
   2. Large type books.
   I. Title
   813.5'2–dc23

ISBN 978–0–7531–9005–0 (pb)

Printed and bound in Great Britain by
T. J. International Ltd., Padstow, Cornwall

Foreword

West Eden was the town's name. Or at least, if one sought upon a very large map at the proper place, he might find in very small type the word, "West Eden." Such was the official designation bestowed many years ago when the village was in its swaddling clothes and without personality.

Since then — from the many personalities making this their home or headquarters and from the hectic days and nights through which it had lived, it had drawn a distinct entity; and, before the green boards upon its scattered shacks had warped and cracked under the first year's sun, men more thoroughly qualified to judge than its optimisitc founders had rechristened it.

It was variously known as Hang Town, Hell's Annex and Temlock's Crossroads. And with the passing years it had won and championed its title to the hardest-little town west of the Atlantic. Which is saying a good deal.

It was the way hereabouts to call into question the propriety of official acts, and a town had no better assurance than a man to keep the name to which he was born. And here, where all the world was in the melting pot, it had no character to be reckoned its own until it had made one for itself. In fifteen years West Eden had grown from a beardless youth of a village into an out-and-out bad man of a town. And it was proud of it and proud of its names. Most frequently was it called Hang Town.

It was a sleepy village of one street, called Main Street as unblushingly as if there had been a dozen other thoroughfares. Main Street was half a mile long. It was crooked and dusty in summer, crooked and muddy in winter. There was a hotel, consisting chiefly of a barroom; there were three stores, with dry goods and groceries in small rooms at the rear and long saloons in front. The post office maintained its grave dignity between two saloons, like a man trying to look sober with a whisky barrel on each side of him.

The census claimed fifteen hundred population, but then the census taker had come into Hang Town at a time when there were races on and a dance scheduled for the evening, and the boys had not told him the truth. Two days later he would have had extreme difficulty in finding five hundred, even if he had counted saddle horses.

A sleepy village during the long summer days, dozing quietly, its empty streets and alleys as sluggish as the arteries of a napping old man — a town of lethargy and languor and empty stores and saloons, very many days and nights of the year. But tonight Hang Town was awake, wide awake.

2

Perhaps it would not have a score of nights like this during the three hundred and sixty-five. Its eyes were open; its lights were on; it was in its holiday clothes.

Men rode this way and that on the one street, calling loudly to their fellows, seeking friends, thirsty perhaps from many days out on the alkali plains of the Bad Country, feverish for a game of draw or stud or a whirl at the wheel, an hour of bucking the tiger. Shod hoofs echoed noisily from the creaking board sidewalks, as sweat-wet cow ponies were spurred all the way up to the swing-doors by some of the more zestful riders. Spur chains and bridle chains jingled and chinked everywhere. And from the hall, named as unblushingly as was Main Street, came the scraping of two fiddles, the thrum of guitar, the clamor of cornet and tinkle of piano, to explain the cause of the foregathering.

CHAPTER
ONE

It was still early. The musicians were just tuning up; the street was filled; the hall was filling. The lines of dusty, sweating saddle horses at the hitching rails lengthened and thickened; the clumping of boot heels on the uneven wooden sidewalk grew into a steady rumble as of distant thunder. Now and then from the cattle country lying to the eastward or from the Bad Country to the west, a cowboy or half a dozen punchers together, from some vast, fenceless cattle spread, clattered into Main Street looking for an evening of frolic.

Naturally, the crowds swelled in the saloons from which later on the jostling throng poured out as from eddying pools in an overflow to the hall. And still, although the music had swung into a waltz and though men came and went, the boots were close together along the the footrails in the barrooms, and the extra bartenders were as busy as their breed likes to be.

In particular, was the Barrel House crowded with vivacious men and girls.

There were in Hang Town, as in all communities where men have built houses and called them their homes, two self-justifying factions. There were the men

4

who unreservedly stood for Temlock, backing up his every play; there were those others who refused to sanction the things he did. And since the Temlock faction was overwhelmingly the stronger, since the Barrel House was known to belong to Temlock, since it was by far the most pretentious saloon in the town, where the biggest games ran their unlimited, unlicensed, open way, it was at the Barrel House that most drinks were sold, most money won and lost.

Here in Hang Town, upon the flank of an unfenced cattle country on the one side, and on the other side the natural gateway into the Bad Country of which most men knew little and that little not good, men were not in the way of troubling themselves about what other men did so long as they themselves were not personally affected. They were a part of a rough country wherein a man, if strong and purposeful, might walk on his heels, if weak and in efficient, must go to the wall.

They were used to living life in the raw as it always pulses where locomotives and electric wires have not found their way; they were content to sit as judges upon their own interests and to look with unprejudiced eyes, aloof and silent, at the happenings just beyond the lines of their property or of their lives.

They had not learned to put faith in law courts and the administrators of the written law. They were slow to step in where they were not personally concerned. And so there were many men in town tonight who were not a declared element of either section — cowboys who knew Temlock or of him, who were not blind to the things which he did, and yet who could not see that it was any of their business.

"He'll get the wrong man some day," was their way of thinking. And then there would be an end of the matter. In the meantime life ran merrily; the games were running full blast; the bartenders were busy; the dance was "livenin' up."

In the Barrel House there was not a man who was not "heeled." Yet nowhere was there hint or sign of a gun. Men, for the most part, wore their coats tonight, there being a little chill in the air for one thing, a coat being an extreme evidence of "dressin' up" for another. And, for those who understand, it is an easy matter for a man to carry a gun, heavy or small calibre as the wearer fancies, under his coattails, in his hip pocket or — again a matter of taste and judgment — in a shoulder holster or in the waistband of his trousers.

Behind the long bar, at the end nearest the snapping doors, was a man whom a stranger never failed to look at sharply, to look at again after his eyes had challenged and been challenged by the bartender's. The man, Henry Lehr, generally known as Long Henery, was not the sort of man one expects to find behind a bar.

He was a very big man, towering high above the two other men aiding him in his labors tonight, so very tall that one had the feeling that he stood on a box. He was always cleanshaven, and his long, heavy jawbone stood out distinctly under the tight-drawn, dead-white of his skin. He was almost bald, although a man of but thirty-five or six, and his forehead, high and broad, seemed an almost abnormally salient feature.

Despite the deadly pallor of the skin, there was no hint of unhealthiness about the man; his eyes, bright, keen, a little small, were like a snake's for brilliancy and alertness. His every gesture bespoke a great, swift, crushing strength. He was a man with a hard reputation, a hard face, a silent tongue. And it was Long Henery who looked after Temlock's interests here in town, who managed the Barrel House and safeguarded the intakings of the till and who, beyond the limits of his duties, attended very strictly to his own business.

Now Long Henery was smiling. He smiled often, laughed very seldom. He was mixing a drink for a newcomer to the saloon, a garrulous, nervous-mannered young fellow who punched cows for the Circle Ten, peddled gossip for the countryside and was known familiarly as Windy Bendish. As usual he was talking.

He had had three or four drinks at the Trail's End Saloon, four or five at the hotel bar, and now had entered announcing joyously that he didn't give a damn for no damn man that didn't give a damn for him.

That was all very well and very good sagebrush philosophy, a very fine thing in its place. And yet it was nobody's business but Windy Bendish's, and it would have been far better for him if he had talked less that night.

Temlock was a man seen very rarely in Hang Town, seen rarely enough anywhere save by those few men whom he trusted to a certain, small extent, and by whom he was watched, cursed and feared. For close to half a year now the village known to so many as Temlock's Crossroads had not caught sight of him or his lean-flanked, roan saddle horse. And because of that, because, further, Temlock was something of a celebrity, it was at once to be judged safe and to be held spectacular for a man to speak as Windy Bendish was speaking. Like many a "little man" before him, he was trying to do something big.

"You ol' hoss thief, you!" he beamed jocularly into Long Henery's smiling face. "What's the word?"

A shaking of the head and a continuance of the smile answered him. Windy Bendish, aware that his entrance had been scarcely noticed, and yearning for something more than that, flung at the urbane bartender:

"I'm lookin' for a man name of Temlock! Know where I can find him?"

The smile remained; the shake of the head was changed to a brief nod. There was no curiosity in Long Henery's expression, no interest in his eyes, no question on his lips.

A few men to whom Bendish's voice carried above the noise of the room turned quickly at the mention of Temlock's name. At the nearest gaming table, where a deft-fingered young man was dealing at draw poker and was being watched very closely by the half dozen men most strongly interested in the fall of the cards, four or five cowboys looking on shifted their eyes to the man standing at the bar.

They were of the Wagon Wheel outfit; they had the habit of traveling together, and they knew a great deal about Temlock. One of them made a low-voiced remark, the others laughed softly and they turned back to watch the game as soon as they saw that it was only Windy Bendish doing the talking.

"Yessir," went on Bendish, his glass poised on the trail to his lips, "I'm lookin' for a man name of Temlock. 'Cause why? 'Cause I've lost a mare better'n which there ain't none trottin' under saddle leather, an' I know where to look for her! 'Cause of all the low-lived hoss thieves as runs loose, there ain't a one crookeder than Temlock! I'm lookin' for him, an' when I find him —"

Any night but this night in the last six months it would have been safe enough for Windy Bendish to say what he pleased about Temlock. But fate is but a game of cards at which the man chiefly interested rarely enough deals. Bendish's glass had not yet gone its brief way to his lips when the door swung back under the impact of an impatient shoulder. He did not notice it, he did not see who it was that had come in. But other men did notice and they saw that the man entering had arrived just in time to hear his name spoken.

Long Henery's quick eyes went to the door, smiling, and came away, smiling. There was no change upon his face; no slightest expression gave any inkling of what he had seen or of what he was thinking. Perhaps he was not thinking at all; perhaps he was not sufficiently interested to remember and mark what he had seen.

9

But one of the men watching the poker game spoke softly; other men turned; the dealer paused in the middle of the deal; an instinctive uneasiness ran down the long barroom until all men turned slowly toward Bendish or the door.

It was a very big man who had entered. As tall as Long Henery, heavier, broader of shoulder, thicker of thigh, Temlock was a man weighing something over two hundred pounds, and as light upon his booted feet as a cat. A great, wide, soft black hat was pushed far back upon his head. His eyes looked with a sort of stony indifference upon the man doing the talking; his lips were drawn back just a little so that the teeth showed. That was Temlock's way of smiling.

For just a moment it was very still in the long barroom. The circling ivory ball at the roulette table spun merrily, its low hum grown suddenly very distinct. Temlock had not spoken, did not speak now, as his eyes went their swift way up and down the room and came again to rest upon Bendish. Then he came a step nearer so that his great bulk no longer stood in the doorway, and a man who had stood just behind him came in with him and stood at his elbow.

This was a man known as widely as Temlock himself; Crag Verilees, a younger man, lean-flanked, clean-muscled, quick-eyed, handsome in a way that was not entirely pleasant, a man with a reputation as far-reaching and as hard as Temlock's. He, too, had heard Windy Bendish's boast and he, too, was smiling. And his smile was at once contemptuous and cruel.

10

Evidently Bendish, who had not yet turned, felt gropingly that something was wrong. He looked curiously into Long Henery's inscrutable face, looked toward the table where the Wagon Wheel boys stood shoulder to shoulder, saw that their eyes had left him and gone steadily toward the door, and then he turned — turned swiftly. Perhaps some sixth sense had told him what to expect.

Temlock was looking him straight between the eyes, Temlock's way. Temlock's brows were drawn a little, his eyes thoughtful. There was no emotion to be read in the hard face; no hint of danger.

But he was thinking, and every man there understood that he must overlook what Bendish had been saying or he must answer it — in just one way.

The cruel eyes of Crag Verilees shifted to his companion's face; the lean, wolfish face of Crag Verilees darkened. He opened his mouth as if to speak and then closed it, saying nothing, shrugging his shoulders.

Almost upon the instant of his turning, Windy Bendish's eyes widened perceptibly; his jaw dropped; his face went a sickly white. The hand holding his glass shook. A little of the fiery liquor spilled upon the bar. He put the glass down noisily.

"So you're lookin' for me, are you, Bendish?" asked Temlock, his voice lingering over his slowly spoken words, a little frown, a little uncertainty still in his eyes. "Well, here I am!"

At least he was not going to overlook what Bendish had said. Several men moved, stepping quietly out of the line of the two, a line which might be defined by a stream of hot lead in a moment. The Wagon Wheel men, their faces very grave, watched Temlock closely. He had made no move to go for his gun; they did not believe that he had quite made up his mind whether or not he was going to kill Bendish.

Bendish had not answered. All of his garrulousness had gone in a second. The man was a coward, and he showed it in his shaking hand, his white face, his staring eyes. His lips moved. His throat made a little dry sound but no words came.

Crag Verilees laughed. His eyes, almost Oriental in their narrow, slanting length, glittered with his hard mirth.

"Come on, Temlock," he said carelessly. "Either go up an' slap the little rabbit or consider it's just the wind ablow-in' as usual an' forget it. I'm thirsty."

"Bendish," said Temlock, his drawl still marked, paying no heed to his friend, "you're just a pore little damn fool. What you say ain't worth listenin' to, an' all the boys knows it. Nor you ain't worth a man's throwin' away good powder an' lead on. Now," and his tone grew just a shade sharper, "you do what I tell you to, an' do it quick. Take up your glass an' drink it, bottoms up, to me. If I was a damn sight worse'n what I am I'd be a better man than you ever was! Drink that!"

Bendish hesitated, looked anxiously into Temlock's stern eyes and from them to the expressionless faces of the men about him.

Again he looked at Temlock; and then he put out a nervous hand, seized the glass and, throwing back his head, tossed the liquor off.

"That settles it," grunted Temlock. He followed Crag Verilees to the bar and slapped down a twenty-dollar gold piece. "The house drinks on me, Henery," he said carelessly. "I ain't been to town for quite some time."

And that would have settled it had Windy Bendish been a wiser man. But someone broke into a short laugh as Bendish drank the compulsory toast, and the laugh and perhaps the simultaneous effect of the brandy, whipped a flush into Bendish's pale face.

Temlock's back was half turned to him. Bendish moved swiftly, his hand flashing to his hip. Long Henery saw and dropped out of sight behind his bar; Crag Verilees saw and stepped a couple of feet to the side; Temlock saw, whirled, drew and fired before Bendish's gun had been raised.

And Bendish dropped, settled and lay still. A snarling, reverberating report, a little puff of smoke, an unerring bit of lead, and "Finis" was scrawled across the inefficient life of Windy Bendish.

His revolver had clattered to the floor close to his out-flung hand; the smoke drifted lazily; thinned and cleared, and Temlock swept the room with his quick eyes, watching for some man to take up Bendish's quarrel. Crag Verilees stood leaning against the bar, the same cruel, contemptuous smile in his eyes as they, too, swept the room.

Long Henery reappeared and stood silent and watchful. No man moved hand or foot for a long silent moment. Then Temlock jammed his gun back into its leather under his coattails.

"I gave him an even break," he said colorlessly. "Better'n an even break. He was just a little fool like I tol' him — his tongue too long, his brain too slow, an' his draw not quick enough. Any of you boys got anything to say?"

Not a man there answered him. Even men who had a mild tolerance almost amounting to a liking for Bendish, and who cordially hated. Temlock, had nothing to say. It had been Bendish's quarrel. He had been the fool that Temlock named him; Temlock had given him more than an even break.

It was finished.

"Come on," said the cool, impudent voice of Crag Verilees. "I'm thirsty. What you drinkin', Temlock?"

And while two men carried Bendish back into a card room and another man went out to find some of his fellows from the Circle Ten, Temlock and Crag Verilees stood at the bar drinking swiftly and deeply.

"He'll get the wrong man some day," muttered Stet Davis, of the Wagon Wheel.

And at that the matter rested.

CHAPTER
TWO

Fifty men had witnessed the occurrence at the Barrel House. Consequently, Con Hathaway, foreman of the Circle Ten and Windy Bendish's boss, had little difficulty in getting the truth of the affair when he arrived ten minutes later. He found the boys from the Wagon Wheel, talked briefly with Stet Davis, shook his head and had nothing to say either to or about Temlock.

The quarrel had been of Bendish's seeking from first to last, inspired by a natural swaggering braggadocio and several drinks. Bendish had not lost a mare, since he had never owned the animal he rode, and, while not a bad sort of fellow, he was absolutely in the wrong this time. So his body was carried to a quiet place for its dreamless sleep and Temlock was allowed to go on his way unquestioned.

It would have been too much to have expected Temlock to show the slightest emotion over the thing which he had done. Little Windy Bendish was not the first man he had killed; never had he shot a man with more semblance of right upon his part.

He remained in the Barrel House for half an hour, drinking a good deal, silent, watchful as was his way, spending his money profligately at the bar which he owned, money that would come back to him through the till and Long Henery's steady fingers.

When they had dulled their thirst he and Crag Verilees moved down along the bar to the gambling tables.

For another half hour they sat into a game of stud poker, making two out of a party of six at one of the tables, playing recklessly from the first card dealt face up. Now Temlock's face was hidden under the broad brim of his hat, now Crag Verilees' wolfish eyes and cruel mouth caught the full light of the lamps as he tilted his own hat far back.

"The black bear an' the lean wolf is huntin' in pairs tonight!" a man said to another watching them.

Of the four other men making up the game at Temlock's table, there was one who seemed out of place here, whose manner, appearance and speech caused him to stand apart from the crowd about him. He had seen the shooting of Bendish, and his fine, intellectual face had whitened and remained white until he had called for brandy and drunk thirstily.

He had played abstractedly until Temlock and Verilees came to the table, watching them furtively all the time, a little look of fear in his eyes. When they did come he looked up at Temlock with a swift question in his glance, muttered a greeting meant to be cordial, half arose and put out a thin, nervous hand.

Temlock ignored the hand as he ignored the greeting, though he dropped into a chair at this man's

16

right hand. There was quick scrutiny, a flashing survey, as his eyes went across the nervous man's features.

He marked in the man's hair the gray that had not been there six months ago, saw that the man looked sixty instead of the fifty that he was, knew that he had had his troubles and his fears, and that he had tried the old, old futile way of drowning them in brandy.

He saw that he was dressed well in "town clothes," and knew from where the money had come. And then he paid no more attention to him until the half hour had passed and he was tired of the game. Then, as with a glance at Crag Verilees and an answering glance from him, Temlock got to his feet, he laid his big hand on his neighbor's arm.

"Come outside, Ellston," he said quietly. "I want to talk to you."

Ellston's face, which had grown a little more placid during the last few minutes, flushed up again, and the old look of fear crept back into his eyes. For a second he seemed about to refuse to go, a something of weak defiance and stubbornness making the fear look like a child's. And then, as Temlock, already half a dozen steps toward the door, half turned and looked at him straight between his eyes, Ellston cashed in his few chips hastily, got to his feet and followed.

As the three men went out through the swinging doors, the man who had remarked about Temlock and Verilees "huntin' in pairs," and who evidently was something of a naturalist in his way, added in a barely audible grunt:

"The black bear an' lean wolf is addin' the jackal to their little party!"

"Who's the white-haired gent?" asked the man to whom he had spoken.

"Him? Why that's Ellston."

"Who's he?"

"Well, he's a Eastern jasper for one thing; he's a weak sister for another; he's a sort of a lawyer nex', an' all aroun' he's a damn little crook. An' havin' talked so much for one evenin' I'm going to have a drink an' go up to the hall an' shake a leg. Come ahead, pardner."

The dance was in full swing when these two had had their drink and came to the hall. The musicians had warmed up to their work. As the first frost of the gathering had thawed before the rising warmth of their merriment, couples greeted one another gaily in swinging past. Brown, brawny men sought out pretty girls in bright-colored homemade gowns, and everywhere in the warm, closely packed room laughter rang out clear and untroubled.

Only a few here had heard of the trouble at the Barrel House, and these few could not see wherein they would be making things better for poor little Windy Bendish by failing to respond to the gala call of the evening. Dances were infrequent in Hang Town; these men and women and girls and boys had come, many of them, long miles.

And the men, those who knew, had much to say to their partners about other things when once their tongues loosened to the music and the whirl of the dance, and saw no need of recounting the tale of a brawl in a saloon and so dampening the joy of the night.

It was not quite ten o'clock when Temlock and Verilees, Ellston following them, came to the door of the hall and stood looking on. Crag Verilees' reason for coming was clear enough. There was no man who rode through the Bad Country who would travel farther to a dance or who was a more graceful dancer when he got there.

Many a girl who had heard mutterings of Crag Verilees' reputation, and who felt a quick distrust on seeing the lean, wolfish face for the first time, forgot her earliest impressions of the man when once she had danced with him. He had a certain rough grace of speech when he chose, a certain humorous way of saying the little things which don't count and yet which do count, and he danced as he did most other things — a bit recklessly, with all his heart, and well.

As for Temlock, every man in Hang Town tonight who knew the man knew that he would come to the dance. Unlike Crag Verilees, he never danced. He did not lift his hat gracefully to a pretty girl. He had in all his life evidenced no desire for society, certainly not the society of women. But he would come just to show himself, just to let men know that he was not afraid after the thing that he had done and that he was not hiding from friends of the man he killed, or from the law.

And Ellston, a man of fifty, had come with them, had followed at Temlock's heels, and men were not surprised. For his face was not the inscrutable, closed book which his companions had learned — if they had not been born with the inherited, instinctive knowledge — to make theirs. He came because Temlock had said bluntly, "Come along!" He came because he was afraid of Temlock, afraid not to come.

When these three men came to the open door to stand there, looking on, Ellston alone hidden a little as he stood behind Temlock and partly in the shadow, Stet Davis, of the Wagon Wheel outfit, was having what he would have termed "the time of his life." He was dancing as Stet Davis knew how, and he was corralling in his long arms the "prettiest, daintiest little lady as ever made a man's heart sorta turn over."

The eyes of many men who were not dancing followed the couple as they spun and raced about the room to the strains of a merry, mad two-step. The eyes of many men who were dancing themselves left their own partners' faces and followed Stet and the girl dancing with him. And it is to be doubted if any of these masculine eyes saw Stet Davis at all.

She had made her own dress out of white and blue stuff. But then, it looked as if it had just grown into a gown to fit her. It showed her arms above the elbow, round and white, dimpled and, seen by masculine eyes, adorable. It showed a glimpse of a throat, of which the same men's eyes were judging in the same masculine adjectives. It showed her ankles twinkling in their thistledown dance in a pair of new blue stockings above a pair of distracting blue slippers with wonderfully high French heels.

The oldest men there judged her to be sixteen; the youngest estimated her age at twenty; the man dancing with her had just coaxed a confession from her and knew that she was going to be nineteen in November. He had even learned the particular day in November — the second — and before he had escorted her to her seat had made up his mind just what he was going to buy for her birthday present.

For Stet Davis knew that she played the violin, and he remembered that in Rocky Bend, only a hundred and seventy-five miles away, there was "the grandest fiddle in the world" for sale at the store, and that it cost only a hundred dollars. Never in all of his carefree existence had Stet Davis had that much money in his hand all at one time. But then such prosaic trifles might well be forgotten and the man forgiven when her gray eyes smiled at his and her red lips curved to laughter at the things he had to say to her.

"Who's that girl?" asked Crag Verilees sharply, as Stet Davis and his laughing partner swung by the doorway.

"That girl!" grunted Temlock. "That's the hell of a nice an' clear description, ain't it, huh? There's only about a hundred females scamperin' about, an' you up an' asks —"

"If there was five hundred girls in this flock," returned Verilees coolly, "you might know which one I'm lookin' at. When I pick out the fairy of the outfit I ain't the kind to waste my time on the rest of the fillies. I mean Bright Eyes with Stet Davis."

Perhaps Temlock had known. At any rate his own eyes had been upon her as Verilees spoke; they followed her as she and Davis passed on and until they were lost across the room.

"I ain't interested none in females," he answered with bluntness.

"Well, I am," laughed Verilee easily, "an' I'm goin' to get my rope on her. She sure can dance!" he approved, as once more his eyes, brightening, lighted upon the girl. "And talk about looks — oh, man!"

Again Temlock, too, was watching her as Stet Davis steered her back within sight. His face darkened just a little at Verilees' words, but his shoulder was turned so that his companion could not see his face. And besides, Crag Verilees would not have seen it just then if it had been turned full upon him. His eyes followed the girl in her every gesture, missed no line of the graceful young body, missed nothing of her eyes' laughter or the laughter of her lips, and as he watched her his interest grew and a certain thoughtful speculation grew with it.

When at last Stet Davis escorted her to her place in the heart of a bevy of laughing girls and smiling elder women at the side of the hall, Verilees swept off his hat, tossed it to a bench beside the door and took a step forward. Temlock, moving swiftly, put out his big hand and laid it heavily upon Verilees' shoulder.

"Where you goin'?" he demanded quickly, his voice dropping a little.

"To get introduced an' to copper the next dance," laughed Verilees.

"Are you a fool?" snapped Temlock.

22

"No. An' I ain't what most folks would call a blind man, neither," reported Verilees. "There don't much grass grow between my toes, Temlock."

Temlock grunted disgustedly.

"It'll be growin' plenty over 'em if you don't look out," he muttered. "I guess you ain't forgot about a man, name of Babe Deveril, of the Two Bar-O, have you, Crag?"

Verilees' face flushed a dark, ominous red.

"Well, what about him?" he asked, shaking off Temlock's hand. "You mean she's his?"

"No," Temlock answered him shortly. "I don't know as he ever seen her. But I do know that he's lookin' for you these days, an' I know he's apt to drift into this town tonight, hearin' there's a dance on. An' if you an' me cut out foolishness an' stick close up to each other, it might be as well for both of us before the sun comes up."

He had spoken swiftly, earnestly, his voice so low that only Verilees and Ellston, craning his neck behind them, caught the guarded words.

Again Crag Verilees laughed his cool, insolent, unpleasant laugh.

"Much obliged, Temlock," he said briefly. "Only I ain't stayin' in the house ever' time Babe Deveril goes out for a walk!"

With that he walked away, seeking the girl who had interested him.

"Who's Babe Deveril? Where's the Two Bar-O?" asked Ellston quickly.

Temlock turned and looked down on him with contemptuous eyes.

"Listenin' again, huh?" he grunted. "Well, if you're so damn curious, Babe Deveril is foreman of a cow outfit, an it's the Two Bar-O, an' it's about one hundred and twenty miles southwest of this. Him an' Crag Verilees has mixed before now an' they're due to mix again — same as oil an' water mixes! One'll go to the top an' one'll go down, way down to hell! I wonder," he added musingly, his sullen eyes going after Verilees, "which one will be up an' which one down?"

Ellston's pale, colorless eyes grew narrow and speculative as he listened.

"What's he done to Babe Deveril?" he asked. "Why is Babe Deveril looking for him?"

Temlock lifted his big, sloping shoulders.

"Don't ask me fool questions if you don't want to get lies for answers," he retorted. "You know I ain't puttin' my foot in other people's affairs much. An' it wouldn't be no grub off'n your plate if you done the same, Ellston. It's Crag's lookout, an' it ain't your'n."

And evidently Crag Verilees was eminently capable of looking after his own destiny. Even in the little matter of getting introduced to a girl who had so swiftly caught his fancy, he showed that. His taut, gaunt form plowed straight through the men and women on the floor, his keen, restless eye now upon the girl where she was gathering her skirts about her to sit down on one of the long benches that flanked the walls, now drifting away in quest of some man who might attend to the necessary social forms for him and introduce him.

24

And while Temlock and Ellston spoke of him and watched him, he found his man, took his arm, steered him straight to where the girl was and bowed not ungracefully in acknowledgment of the brief presentation.

Temlock was deep in a brooding silence. Ellston opened his mouth, began to say something, saw Temlock's face turned darkly upon him and swallowed his words. And a moment later, when a quadrille was announced, they saw Crag Verilees offer the girl his arm, saw her slip her hand through it and move with him to their place.

Throughout the dance Temlock did not move from the door, nor did he once speak. He found tobacco and papers and with big, slow, steady fingers rolled a cigarette. He watched the crowd of dancers when the music struck up, his eyes running back and forth, stopping oftenest, resting longest, upon Crag Verilees and his pretty partner.

Verilees was talking easily to her, bending over her, and she was laughing at something he was saying. Then came the command to "Swing your pardners!" and the two whirled away amidst the bright-colored, gay throng.

Still Temlock stood silent, watching; still Ellston at his side was silent and watched with him. They saw Verilees' tall form, saw the white and blue of the girl's dainty gown, her broad sash flying, glimpsed the gleam of a smile upon the man's sinister face, and again Ellston began abruptly, irritably, to speak.

"Shut up!" growled Temlock. "Come outside. I'm thirsty an' besides, like I tol' you a while ago, I got something to say."

Ellston followed him, looking at him curiously. Temlock, walking swiftly, his great strides making it difficult for the smaller, slighter man to keep up with him, led the way back to the Barrel House. They met many men as they passed along the noisy street, and the men whom they met seemed to see Temlock alone, not to note the other. Some said, "Hello, Temlock!" briefly; some did not speak at all; all eyed him sharply. And he, with no nod, no single word in greeting to any of them, went his swift, straight way, his hat low over his eyes, his big fingers flattening the cigarette which already he had allowed to go out.

CHAPTER
THREE

At the saloon Long Henery served them, his silence as profound as Temlock's, his eternal smile masking whatever he might be thinking. The two men drank; drank again at Ellston's invitation; drank a third time at Long Henery's. Then Temlock led the way to the rear of the building, to the little card room where earlier in the evening the body of the man he had killed had lain.

"Now, Ellston," he said abruptly, having closed the door and disposed his big body loosely upon the table — the same table upon which gentle hands had put Windy Bendish. "You know me, an' you know damn well that when I want a thing I get it!"

Ellston, his manner showing the same nervousness, the same hint of fear it had shown when for the first time that night he had seen Temlock, remained standing, now and again forcing his faded eyes to meet Temlock's scowl, now and then dropping them to the foot which toyed with a broken poker chip.

"Well," Temlock flung at him after a moment of silence, "what do you stan' there like a deef mute for? Didn't you hear me?"

"Yes," answered Ellston, his face flushing, the white hand at his side shutting tight with a little passing spasm of anger. "You know I do."

"You act like you was afraid if you opened your mouth I'd pick the gol' out'n your teeth!" snarled Temlock. "I didn't come to town just to get drunk tonight, Ellston, and I didn't come to make a fool of myself at a shindig. I come on business an' I come to see you!"

"Me?" Ellston's eyes flew open in surprise, and the fear in them stood up high and unhidden.

Temlock laughed shortly.

"You little coward, you," he jeered. "You ain't got the insides of a sheep dawg. But you listen jus' the same."

He leaned forward on the table, pushing his hat far back for once so that Ellston might look into his eyes, and for a moment stared at him in a dark, musing silence. When again he spoke, his voice carried no farther than it was meant to carry, only as far as Ellston's ears. But still Ellston looked nervously toward the closed door and put out his shaking hand as if to stay the flow of words.

"I got you where I want you, ain't I?" jeered Temlock. "Most things I do, I do pretty much in the open an' I don't care a damn if folks has a right smart guess about it. An' you —" a strange, deep scorn made his low-toned words vibrate — "you crawl an' hide an' sneak an' lie — an' what good's it did you? In a minute, before I'm gettin' a good start sayin' what I got to say, you'll come so close to faintin' that most likely I'll have to go out an' get a flask of whisky to keep you standin' up!"

Already Ellston's pale face had gone a deathly white; already he looked the part of a man about to faint. He pulled himself up, returned Temlock's look a long, wavering moment, then weakened and dropped into a chair, his face going into his shaking hands.

"For God's sake —" he began.

"Cut it!" commanded Temlock angrily. "Don't start whimperin.' You can do your prayin' tomorrow, after I'm gone."

Ellston looked up quickly, a quick light in his eyes which Temlock saw and understood and which drove a more stinging sneer into his words as he went on mercilessly.

"I've took a good deal of trouble with you, Ellston," he continued. "A sight of bother, first an' last, figgerin' I'd use you later on. Like I have already," he added significantly, with a little pause after the words. "Like I'm goin' to now, which I hadn't figgered on original. I've took more trouble than you know, Ellston. Now, to make sure you don't make no mistakes, I'm goin' to tell you about it. I doped it out a long time ago that this here was a funny place for a man like you to come to live. So I got busy an' found out why!"

Ellston's hands were tight-clenched; his lips moistened each other continually. But he made no answer.

"I know you come from a little town in Marylan'," went on Temlock presently. "I know you was a cashier of a bank there before you come out here and turned lawyer. I know why you left in a hurry. A man as can't gamble no more successful than you, Ellston, an' that can't drink no better, had oughta left both of them habits out'n his day's work."

"Damn you!" gasped Ellston.

Temlock's lips drew back just a little so that the teeth showed in Temlock's smile. There was no other change of expression as he looked Ellston straight between the eyes, no change in his voice as he said quietly:

"Don't forget yourself, Ellston! I know you got a gun on your hip an' I know you'd like to use it. But you just remember what happened to Windy Bendish!"

He saw that Ellston heard, understood, remembered. And then he went on:

"My trouble paid, huh? I can sen' you back where you're wanted most, Ellston, an' you know it. More'n that, I've got the deadwood on you for more'n one job you've did for me. They don't like forgers much in this state," he said dryly. "Not much more'n they like cow rus'lers. Maybe not so much."

"You made me do it," muttered Ellston."

"Sure. Not so much because I had to have it done as because it would put you where I'd have you when I did want you, where I'd have the deadwood on you, like now. I figgered it might come in handy some day to have a law crook on my side."

"Well," cried Ellston, "what do you want? I'll do it!" He laughed, a weak, mirthless laugh and ran his hand across his dry lips. "I don't care what it is, I'll do it. My God, I can't help myself now!"

"That's the proper talk," said Temlock, eying him with blended curiosity and contempt.

"Well," cried Ellston impatiently, "what is it? Why don't you tell me and get it over with? Put a name to it, man!"

"I'm goin' to. Only —" with slow emphasis — "I wanted you to get it into your head good an' clear first that you're goin' to do it, an' it don't make no speck of difference what it is. It's just like you says: you're goin' to do it!"

He paused a moment, taking time to make a fresh cigarette, lighting it, looking at Ellston's drawn face through the first puff of smoke.

And then suddenly it came.

Temlock, suddenly tense, leaned forward and said harshly:

"I never saw but one woman I wanted for mine. I've foun' her now, an' God Himself, couldn't keep her out'n my hands, Ellston, an' sure not a little shrimp like you! An' that woman —"

"Well?" with swift suspicion.

"Is the one Crag Verilees was dancin' with — him!"

"Not — not my little girl! Not Marian!"

"I wouldn't say she was yours, to look at her," returned Temlock with scant courtesy. "Nor yet to talk with her. A man wouldn't believe a gent' like you, Ellston, could have a kid like her. But —"

"Are you crazy, Temlock?" Ellston sprang to his feet, the blood flowing into his cheeks. "You must be crazy!"

"Yes, I'm crazy," Temlock assured him gravely. "I always said a man was crazy when he let a fool woman come in an' upset his style of life, which that girl has certainly did with me. Now, you just go on listenin' a spell longer. That's your game this trip.

"I've saw lots of females in my day an' never lost any sleep rememberin' what they looked like. Then I run acrost your girl. That's three years ago, Ellston, an' I ain't forgot it yet. An' I've saw her more times than one since, and she's sorta always stuck in my mind. Last time was six months ago, an' I went away cussin' myself for a fool, an' I got drunk to shet her out'n my mind, an' I swore I wasn't goin' to waste my time throwin' my bran' on no little white heifer that ever strayed acrost my trail.

"An' the next mornin' I woke up rememberin' the color of her eyes an' the way she did her hair with a flower in it, an' how she looked when I seen her playin' her fiddle, it all cuddled up against her face, an' I've rode some considerable since then an' I ain't forgot a damn bit of it! That's why I come back tonight — because she dragged me back! Crazy?" He laughed in short self-disgust. "Of course I'm crazy. An' when I seen Stet Davis puttin' his arms aroun' her, an' then Crag —"

He broke off suddenly, his face crimson, his big hands clenched. Slowly he slipped from the table, towering high above Ellston, and his voice was shaky and husky as he said:

"I've got to have her! I'm goin' to have her! I'm goin' to kill any man as tries to keep me away from her! An' — an' she'd be afraid of me at first. That's where you come in, do you hear me, Ellston? I've got the deadwood on you an', by God Ellston, I'm man enough

32

to use what tools are put into my hands! You've got to get her for me. Understand?"

Ellston stared at him incredulously.

"You're crazy, Temlock," he muttered. "Crazy and drunk. Think what you are saying! If I wanted to do this thing, how in heaven's name could I? You might as well ask for the moon!"

"How?" snarled Temlock. "You ask me how?"

Then suddenly his great hands shot out. They gripped Ellston's throat, they closed tight, tighter, and they sank their fingers into the flesh. And then as suddenly, Temlock threw the man away from him. Ellston's trembling body struck against the board partition separating the card room from the main room of the saloon, and he stood there cowering, his face dead-white again, his hands going to his throat, the fear of death in his eyes.

Temlock followed him, coming across the room, thrusting his blazing eyes close down to Ellston's.

"Maybe I'm both crazy an' drunk," he said harshly, his deep chest rising and falling to a great intake of air. "Suppose I am? That don't make no difference in your play. You can make her do it; you can drive her to it; you can scare her to it. You can tell her what I'll do to you if you don't. I'll disgrace you first, an' — I'll kill you next."

Ellston shivered and drew back, his body tighter pressed against the wall.

"I — I'll try," he gasped. "Tomorrow —"

"Tonight! An' you bet you'll try!"

Temlock threw open the door and went out. Ellston hesitated and followed, perhaps through force of habit. It was habit with Ellston to follow.

Temlock went to the bar and Long Henery passed out the bottle. Temlock drank, then jerked his head toward Ellston who put out a shaking hand for his glass. Temlock went out alone.

Ellston remained at the bar, drinking.

CHAPTER
FOUR

Just before midnight Old Man Adams, the spry, nimble, perennially young graybeard who had called "Swing your pardners!" and "Grand right and left!" and "All promenade!" for the square dances, in many a cow town at many a frolic, and without whom no dance within many a mile of this ebullient town would have been quite perfect, sang out:

"Supper dance! Take your pardners for the supper dance!"

Men made beelines toward their girls. The laughing, flushed, happy Marian Ellston became the focal point for several hopeful males. Some had already asked for the supper dance and some hadn't got around to it, what with one thing and another. At the fore were Stet Davis and Crag Verilees. On the well-greased floor, slick with candle shavings, these two slid up to her like men on ice skates.

"My dance! It's mine, remember, Miss Marian!" said Crag Verilees, at her side about one step ahead of Stet Davis. He started to take her into his arms.

Laughing, she drew back.

"You did say something about it, I believe, Mr Verilees," she retorted, very gay. "But that was just as the next dance was starting and I didn't have a chance to tell you —"

Stet Davis looked Crag Verilees up and down in a fashion to suggest that Mr Stet Davis of the Wagon Wheel spread didn't have any particular fondness for Mr Crag Verilees or anyone like him.

"Better luck somewheres else, Verilees," he said as he offered his arm to the girl. "This young lady came to the dance with me, she's havin' supper with me an' I'm takin' her home when the dance is over."

Crag Verilees ignored him but jerked up his eyebrows at the girl.

"Really, I have promised this dance to Mr Davis," she told him with a bright nod, and slipped into Stet's arms.

Crag Verilees stood there appraising her with eyes in which his admiration stood high; a look like that couldn't displease any girl, especially when it came from a man as handsome, as interesting looking as Verilees. Moments like this made a girl's evening a sort of dream, stitched through with thrills. Verilees said as his eyes continued to flatter her:

"You be sure to save me the secon' dance after supper! You will, won't you, Miss Marian?"

She flashed a swift glance up into Stet Davis' darkening face; it was fun to tease him a bit; she nodded and smiled back at Crag Verilees and said a quick, "Yes; I'll remember and save it for you."

Stet Davis swung her clean off her dancing feet.

"I don't like that Verilees, Marian," he told her, and his voice sounded as though it came through clenched teeth. "You better not have anything to do with him; you better not dance with a man like him."

She simply couldn't quite take anything seriously tonight, not with the lights and the beat of the music and the bright laughter all about her, with all the pretty girls in billowing, colorful dresses, the young fellows in their holiday best.

She gasped, "Don't squeeze me to death, Stet!" And when he realized that that was just exactly what he was doing, and relaxed the hard muscles of his arms, she tip-tilted her flowerlike face and lifted her big, mirth-brimming eyes up to his somber ones and said, pretending demureness: "But he's so terribly handsome, Stet! And he's really awfully nice. And he dances perfectly divinely!"

She hadn't known Stet Davis very long; she didn't know him so terribly well, but she liked him. And it was fun, a sort of impish fun, to plague him. Oh, not really to hurt him, but just to tease him and watch the changing light in his eyes.

Stet Davis grunted. He said:

"So's a rattlesnake nice to look at, if you like that sort of thing, and I've heard folks say as how a rattlesnake, crawlin' through the grass, is as graceful as all get-out, if you're of a mind for that kind of gracefulness. I tell you, Crag Verilees is no good, and it don't do any nice girl like you any good to be seen even sayin' howdy to him, let alone dancin' with him."

"What did he ever do to you, Stet?"

"Come on, let's dance," muttered Stet, and began flinging his feet.

Then the musicians, warm and thirsty, stopped in the middle of a beat; their eyes, rolling sideways, were on the clock high on the wall. It was midnight. Time out for supper.

Marian's gay eyes kept drifting; she saw Crag Verilees across the room and he smiled at her and she smiled back. His eyes were bold, almost predatory, and her eyes were warm and happy, almost coquettish. She saw him offer his arm to the girl he was dancing with, a very young girl, maybe sixteen, and pretty, a girl with yellow hair tied with a big blue ribbon, with rounded baby-blue eyes — a plumply rounded girl, the type that the countryside termed, without seeking a more elegant way of saying it, "corn-fed." Marian knew her; it was Sally Freeman, a good-humored, kind-hearted, empty-headed little ninny. Cuddlesome, though, and cute and a lovely dancer.

The laughing, jostling couples streamed out through the hall's double doors and onto the street that was lighted by the stars and the mellow glow pouring out from many an open saloon door and window. In the warm human press at the doors, Marian, clinging to Stet Davis' arm to be safely carried through, overheard scraps of talk between two men; they were just behind her, almost at her shoulder. One was saying:

". . . and that ended it up. One shot done it. Little Windy Bendish has did his last blowin' off of steam here or anywheres else."

The other man said carelessly:

"Temlock, huh? Temlock shot him?"

"Well, Windy asked for it; for once you couldn't blame Temlock. He come in along with Crag Verilees. The two of 'em —"

Those within the doorway burst out upon the sidewalk; others of the churning couples thrust in between, and that was all that she heard. Her fingers tightened on her escort's arm.

"Stet!" she whispered. "Did you hear? There's been trouble tonight! Temlock killed poor little Windy Bendish!"

"You can't help things like that happenin'," said Stet Davis tolerantly. "You know that. All you got to do is just forget it. Let's step out and grab our plates while the grabbin' is good!"

He hurried her almost into a run; everybody was hurrying.

"But you knew about it, Stet? You had already heard about it? When did it happen? Just now? While — while we were dancing and laughing in there?"

"Now, don't you let it fuss you. No, it happened before, before we started dancin'. Now, don't let it get to botherin' you."

"And Crag Verilees was there when it happened — he saw it happen! And then he came straight over to the dance, and in a minute or two he forgot all about it! Forgot that a man had just been shot to death before his eyes! And by a friend of his!" Her breath caught. "And, you Stet!"

"I ain't shot nobody, not tonight anyway," he grunted back at her. "Come, let's scoot! First served is best served in this man's town."

"But with a man just killed — not dead more than a few minutes! And then to go to a dance!"

"He won't be any deader, come seven years, than he is right now. Pick up your feet, Marian; get it out of your head. Here we go!"

She didn't say anything more. She glanced up at the stars, and they looked immeasurably far away; she glanced into the Barrel House, and the light pouring out was warm and yellow, and lapped them about intimately. She looked swiftly at Stet Davis' face; it looked stern, hard, unyielding despite all his light talk.

The supper provided for the dance crowd in this little rollicking town was a sort of midnight picnic. It was served at long tables improvised from planks resting on sawhorses in the schoolhouse from which all desks had been moved and stacked up outside to provide room. The plank tables, flanked by rough benches, were covered with cloths of various sizes and hues, white for the most part but with a sprinkling of warmer colors. Huge platters were piled high with fried chicken, roast chicken, stewed chicken; there were brown, crusty pies to make a man's mouth water, to turn a loose-footed cowboy into a domestic animal; there were salads and pickled peaches and watermelon rind preserves and jellies and jams and cakes, as likewise there were the humbler potatoes and carrots and onions. It was rumored that presently several ice-cream freezers were sure to disgorge their contents in full, unstinted measure. And flanking the board were a score of the community's young matrons along with some not so very young who had had a finger in this sort of pie for many and many the year, all of them flush-faced and smiling and eager — and proud of their individual contributions to the feast.

The acknowledged job and responsibility of every swain was to steam ahead, to elbow the way for his lady, to make sure that she was seated and strategically placed. Stet Davis knew his duty well, and with Marian Ellston in his wake, plowed straight ahead, his single-purposed eye upon a site not already pre-empted at one of the long tables. He put his big hands about her slim waist and lifted her up and over the bench and set her down — and as he did so, Crag Verilees came steering his own purposeful way with the smiling, downy Sally Freeman hanging onto his sleeve, and he placed Sally and himself — and made sure that he was elbow to elbow with Marian Ellston.

"Say, this is great!" said Crag Verilees. "Here we are, together again! It's in the cards!"

There was nothing that Stet Davis could do about it. Sally leaned back and said behind Crag Verilees' high, lean shoulders, "Hello, Marian!" and Marian smiled back at her, and said, "Hello, Sally. Having a good time?" And Sally said, with a deep breath, her eyes evincing a tendency toward an upward roll, "Grand!"

Stet Davis' long arms stretched out over the table.

"How do you like your chicken, Marian?"

"Oh, it all looks so good, doesn't it?"

He heaped her plate as though he were feeding a farm hand — a second joint of golden brown fried chicken, a piece of breast of roast chicken, a big spoonful at random of stewed chicked. He dragged in mashed potatoes and gravy —

He made her gasp and laugh.

"Stet Davis! Do I look as hungry as all that?"

There was much calling back and forth across the long tables and up and down from one end to the other as young people discovered friends and waved and voiced their greetings which had to be guessed at in all the uproar rather than heard word for word. During all this, Crag Verilees made rather a point of ignoring his supper partner and striving to monopolize Marian Ellston. For a time she withdrew as into a shell; in her overstimulated mind was the picture of that great brute of a man, Temlock, shooting little Windy Bendish to death, with an arrogant, aloofly interested Crag Verilees looking on, and for a few minutes she shrank away from his nearness, instinctively frightened. It was good, just then, to have Stet Davis on her other side.

But everyone was so gay, so full of high spirits, and the speeding moment was so electric — and, after all, it hadn't been Crag Verilees who had killed a man tonight — some few minutes or short hours ago. And Verilees was insistent, and his obvious interest flattered a young girl — and it was fun to tease good old Stet Davis just a little bit.

"It's a funny thing, Miss Marian," Crag Verilees was saying to her, his voice lowered in a confidential sort of way as, ignoring Sally Freeman, he strove to have her ignore her escort, "how, though I've heard of you, of course, and all that, I never once put my eyes on you until tonight! Why didn't anybody ever tell me as how

42

you're the prettiest girl that ever was? You just listen to me: You're goin' to see a whole lot more of me from now on!"

She glanced at Stet Davis. Yes, he had heard every word of it. She saw his jaw harden; she saw that his eyes could harden, too. And it dawned on her that this cowboy from the Wagon Wheel was not a person for anyone, man or woman, to trifle with.

Marian leaned back, reached behind Verilees and tapped the deserted Sally on the shoulder.

"Move over next to me, Sally," she invited. "I want to talk to you."

That would put Sally between her and Verilees. But Verilees would have none of it.

"You're all right where you are, ain't you Sally?" he demanded. "Sure you are. You an' Miss Marian can do your talkin' when we get back to the hall." And he even bethought himself to say belatedly, "More chicken, Sally?"

Sally brightened at being briefly noticed.

"That cream pie looks awful good, don't it, Crag?"

There was a rough, innate chivalry deeply implanted in Stet Davis' heart. He yearned to batter all the insolent good looks off Crag Verilee's face; so throbbing with desire was that urge that he found it all but impossible to restrain his heady impulse, yet it remained that he was with Marian Ellston and he did not want the evening to degenerate into a public brawl — over her. For everyone would know what impelled him if he let himself go —

Marian felt the tension. As sharp as a slap in the face came the realization that she was going too far in this light game of hers, just having fun making Stet Davis mildly jealous. The look she surprised on Stet's face as he dragged his eyes away from Crag Verilees was one of stormy hatred. She shivered; back to her excited fancies came the picture of what had just happened at the Barrel House. Men, moved mightily, killed one another. She had never thought of Stet Davis as a potential killer — but what, when you stripped them down to the raw, were all these men?

She strove to catch hold of the moment, to direct its trend, to manage it with a certain adroitness. She took a deep breath; she said, making a long sigh eloquent:

"Oh, it was the best supper, Stet! Do you think we can ever dance again, after eating like this? — Hello, Mrs Thompson!" She waved across the table to a jolly, middle-aged woman. "That was the best chicken! Oh, I could tell you cooked it!" And, coming back to Stet Davis: "Hadn't we better run? They'll be dancing again and we'll miss the first dance!"

Crag Verilees was up before Stet Davis was.

"So long as we don't miss the second dance, Miss Marian!" Then he caught Sally Freeman by the elbow. "Here we go, Sally."

"But my pie!" wailed Sally.

"Oh, you can eat pie most any day. An' you don't look much starved to me anyhow."

Sally pouted prettily, but he didn't notice.

The four got up. Stet Davis touched Marian's elbow and they made their way out. Right at their heels came the other couple, Crag Verilees hurrying little Sally Freeman.

And they started up the street four abreast, Stet Davis, Marian — and next to Marian, Crag Verilees with Sally hanging to his outside arm.

Stet Davis stopped abruptly. Verilees stopped.

"What are we stoppin' for, Stet?" asked Verilees in that half-sneering, good-natured way of his. The man could be either as smooth as silk or as rough as emery, just as he chose.

Stet Davis didn't look at him. He said very quietly to Marian:

"Will you two girls run ahead? I've got a couple of words to say to Verilees here. I'll be right along."

"No, Stet! No!" She caught his arm tight in both hands. "Please! Let's hurry. We don't want to miss our first dance!"

Stet Davis had been more than merely patient all evening; he wasn't used to riding himself with a curb bit and a tight rein. She saw a little flicker as of red fire in his eyes; his voice was still quiet but it was like the heavy silence when you await a clap of thunder.

"Do like I say; you and Sally run ahead. I'm with you in two shakes."

Sally had heard and came hurrying to Marian's side, flinging an arm about her, saying in her giddy way:

"Oh, come along, Marian! The two great big he-men want to be alone a minute." She giggled. "Maybe they want to sneak acrost the road and have a coupla drinks. Leave 'em have it."

Marian was in despair. Yet with Stet Davis looking at her like that she couldn't do anything but move along with Sally. They didn't run; Marian's high heels dragged; she kept looking back.

"What's all this, Stet?" said Crag Verilees in his confident, mocking sort of way.

"I've got a bellyful of you tonight, Verilees," said Stet Davis. "But, as far as that goes, I always did have a bellyful of you. From now on, lay off. Understand?"

Crag Verilees laughed. His eyes were following the two loitering girls.

"You don't much fancy how your little new heifer looks at me, huh, Stet? You're scared that when I get her in my corral an' slap my brand on her an' —"

Stet Davis' clenched fist caught him full in the sneering mouth. Crag Verilees rocked on his heels and went staggering back. He steadied himself and stared at his assailant, a look of surprise stamping itself on his arrogant face. He wiped his mouth on the back of his hand.

"Why, you —"

He was nearly half a dozen inches taller than the compact Stet Davis; he was rangy and long-armed and all whipcord and resilient steel. And he was exploding with murderous rage.

He laughed, and his laughter was free, unfettered, exultant. Here was just what he had wanted all night! He tore into the smaller man like a landslide bearing down on a sapling.

And he ran into more flying hard-knuckled fists than he had ever realized one man could command. Stet

Davis, too, had been hungering for this moment. Again he caught Crag Verilees full upon the already battered mouth. He accepted a tremendous blow on the jaw and did not even know that he shook his head; he was not conscious of feeling anything.

He lashed out, both fists flailing, and beat into Crag Verilees' belly until the tall man began to sag and double up. He took another swinging blow in the face but kept on, hard at work like an old-fashioned battering-ram that didn't know anything but to batter, that didn't feel anything.

Crag Verilees gathered himself for a blow meant to kill or half kill the other man. But he didn't deliver it quite soon enough; he gave himself an extra tenth part of a second. In that he made his mistake.

Stet Davis lifted a hard fist from low down and brought it up like something shot out of a gun to land square on the proper spot on Crag Verilees' jaw. Whereupon the taller man folded up from heel to crown; his knees sagged, his eyes grew vacant — he didn't know what had hit him.

Stet Davis stood a minute looking down at him. Then he dusted off his knuckles and went ahead to rejoin his dance partner.

CHAPTER
FIVE

With an hour off for supper, it was exactly one o'clock when the dancers came streaming back into the hall. The fiddler was already making a good deal of preparatory noise, tuning up; lamps that had been turned low were turned up again, and the dance went on, pulsing and thrilling with a mirth and swing that long ago had been entirely thawed and were genuine and unfettered.

Sally Freeman lingered near the door, waiting for a man who didn't trouble even to remember her. Stet Davis and Marian danced together, the first after-supper dance. She looked up at him swiftly, penetratingly, anxiously; she parted her lips to say something, then kept still. She saw the glint in his eyes, the rough reddening along his jaw; she knew something had happened between him and Crag Verilees — she knew pretty well what it was. She hadn't exactly seen, but almost! A crowd had swept in between her and the two men. She saw that Stet Davis was bruised, and somehow she knew that Crag Verilees carried a more battered and less arrogant face. She didn't know what to say. So, wiser girl than she knew, she didn't say anything.

48

They danced and were happy with all the rest of the happy throng.

Crag Verilees did not return to the dance hall. Brooding, his wrath smoldering, in no mood for such jocular quips as were bound to come his way when men noticed his battered lips, he went his dark, solitary way to the Barrel House where for an hour he played carelessly at the faro table, winning enough to "make wages," and drinking a good deal of whisky.

At four o'clock some of the boys at the dance, tireless and "jus' gettin' warmed up," drew down the window shades to shut out the coming day and went about among their fellows making up a little purse to keep the musicians good-natured and at their posts. It was noted that Stet Davis yielded up what the night had left in his pockets and that he did so grinning broadly.

But at last, it was after five o'clock; the sun was up in the cloudless sky, and the dance broke up as dances must. The last waltz, the "Home Sweet Home," drawn out in slow cadences of lingering regret, the rising of many voices, men's and women's to the old, old air, a little tightening of arms about slim waists, gentle pressures of little hands in return, and the dance was over.

Stet Davis, seeing Marian Ellston home, walked as slowly as Stet Davis knew how, and cattle men are not famed for swiftness on foot. But at last Main Street lay behind; they had come to a little cottage set in a flower garden; the gate had creaked to his hand; he had said good morning at the top step; the gate had creaked again as he went out, and Ellston's daughter went swiftly into the house.

Her cheeks were still flushed from the dance, her eyes bright with the happiness of one of Hang Town's few social gatherings. She opened the door of the small living room, saw that a lamp was still burning on the rickety table, disputing with its weak rays the golden light of the sun, turned the wick down and moved slowly toward her little bedroom. And then for the first time she was aware that her father was sitting in a big chair in a corner of the room, eying her with a peculiar expression in his eyes which she could not understand, which in a vague way alarmed her.

"What is it, father?" she asked quickly. She stopped abruptly and stood very still, looking down at him, wondering. Why should he be up and sitting here at this hour? It was not his way to sit here alone when he came in late at night, or early in the morning.

For a moment he did not answer. His eyes clung to her face, frowning, low-lidded, studying her.

She laughed a little uneasily.

"You look at me as though you were trying to make up your mind what sort of a young lady I am!"

"Maybe that is what I am doing," he answered her.

She bit her lip and a little shadow of pain contracted her brows. A certain thickness in the man's words told her what he had been doing while she was at the dance. And there was that look in his eyes which puzzled her — a look which she had never seen there even while Ellston's drinking was heaviest.

"Sit down," he commanded curtly. He had grown restless under her searching regard and angry with her because of it. "I want to talk to you."

"Hadn't we better wait until later, father?" she said gently. "It's so late, and I'm sleepy. We're both sleepy."

She could think of nothing that he need say now. No doubt, she thought bitterly, it was some trifle which the alcohol had magnified into importance, something which he would forget when he had slept.

"No," he told her briefly. "I have waited for you to come in. I've waited for hours — all night. I want to talk with you now."

Not only was there something in the man's facial expression to cause her to wonder, but an odd note in his voice made her perplexity grow. Not that it was curt and hard; she was quite used to unpleasant words from him. But there was a quality of tone that mystified her, that, though vaguely, alarmed her.

Making no reply now, she sank into the chair by which she was standing and watched him, waiting for him to go on.

"Damn it, girl!" he cried irritably. "Don't look at me like that — like I was some wild animal you'd never seen before!"

She dropped her eyes and lowered her lids to humor him, but not so that she failed to see him whip a flask out from his coat pocket and drink swiftly before he went on. Now all of the sparkle of happiness had gone out of her eyes, the glowing pleasure-flush fading from her cheeks. The dance with its tinseled gaiety, which was none the less gay, was a thing of some long ago, dead like ashes in a fireplace. She was back in a sordid home with a man whom it was her duty to love.

"Marian," he began now, his tone curter, harder, his little air of uneasiness washed away with the sip of brandy, "it has been hard, God knows, out here in this wild country to rear a daughter as a daughter of mine should be reared. And yet, I have done my best. I have sent you to school when other men's daughters were in the kitchen or milking cows and feeding pigs. I have given you the best education circumstances would allow. I have done my best, Marian, to make you happy and to make you a cultured, refined woman. I have done my best, Marian," he repeated sharply, as if defying argument on the subject.

Her head drooped a little lower; she hid her eyes entirely from him. A daughter should love her father, should revere her father, should not hold her father in contempt! And how well, deep down in her heart, the girl knew that he had done nothing for her, that it had been her mother to whom she owed all that she was, a mother who had struggled with life until her only child was almost a woman, who clung loyally to a husband who had lost all illusion for her, and who then had died broken-hearted, broken-spirited, utterly wretched at the end of an utterly wretched life.

"Never once have I asked you to do a thing of importance for me; never have I commanded," went on Ellston in a tone which made the girl wonder if the man actually believed the thing he was saying. "And now, what I am going to suggest is prompted entirely by my love of you, by my sincere wish to see you placed in a position where your happiness will be assured."

He paused, gathering his words for what was to come. She could not help looking at him now, swiftly, wonderingly. What was this thing which, like all things which he suggested, would benefit not her, but him?

"You are going to be twenty soon, Marian," he said.

"Nineteen, father," she reminded him with a queer little smile. Why should she expect him to remember how old she was when he so seldom remembered her birthday? "It doesn't matter, though."

"Well, nineteen," he retorted sharply. "No, it does not matter. The thing that does matter is that you are a woman now. You are old enough to be married!"

"Married!" she gasped.

"Yes." He ran a dry tongue along his dry lips. "Married. I have been thinking of this a long time, Marian. I — I have always planned ahead for your welfare. And — I have found the man who is in every way suited to insure your happiness."

"You — have — found —"

She broke off, wordless, breathless, all but stunned by the mental shock of his words.

Then more quietly, speaking with slow distinctness, she went on:

"I have no wish to marry, father. I have never seen the man whom I could care enough for — that way — to marry. You see," she said, trying to speak lightly, striving to smile at him, "this is a thing which fathers nowadays leave to their daughters. I shall know the prince when he comes, father!"

The door behind her father's chair creaked a little; it seemed to her that someone was leaning against it, listening, in the next room, her father's bedroom. But she noted the fact vaguely, subconsciously, and it made little impression upon her otherwise busy mind at the time.

"You have more sense than most girls, Marian," Ellston ran on quickly. He too had heard the slight sound and he knew who was listening. "Now is the time to use it. You've got to marry some day, and then you've got to choose wisely and not let your fancies run away with your sane judgment. Where other girls would run after a young fellow for what he has in his face and on the tip of a lovemaking tongue, you've got to choose a man for what he has in his head and, yes, in his pocket. There's no use being a fool, my girl."

"Who is this man whom you have selected for me?" she asked quietly, shutting the bitterness out of her voice, trying desperately to drive the contempt from her eyes and from her heart.

"I want to tell you about him first," evaded Ellston. "He is older than you, but not too old. A girl should marry a man older than herself. He is not the kind to dangle after a girl and make pretty speeches. He is a man of big interests, of large responsibilities, a very busy business man."

"So far he doesn't sound very interesting," she said as gently as she could. "Not to a girl, father."

"Let me finish!" he cried angrily. "You're a fool if you are not interested! He is the richest man within five hundred miles of us! When — when in a short time, a year or so from now, he gives up his business and retires, he is going to be in the position to give his wife everything in the world she could ask for — dream of!"

"Even love, father? Or are you forgetting that?"

"I am forgetting nothing. Love? That is the fool's way to spell nonsense with four letters, girl! Leave love alone. It will come."

"But the man? Are you going to tell me who he is?"

"Yes. He is — It's Temlock!"

Her face went red, fiery-red with the wild rush of blood to it. And then it went white, dead-white with pain, horror, unhidden disgust.

"Temlock!" She repeated the name after him, flinging the word at him in hot disdain as she rose to her feet. "Temlock! You come to me and ask me to marry a man like Temlock! Father" — the voice which had shaken a little was very steady now, very low, very distinct — "if you ever so insult me again, whether you are sober or not sober, I am going to leave this place we have called home and go as far away as a good God will let me!"

She passed him swiftly, going to her room. He got to his feet as quickly, though not so steadily, and his hot hand grasped her arm.

"Where are you going?" he cried. "Listen to me!"

"I am going to bed," she returned, trying to slip her arm out of his tense grasp. "I do not wish to listen to you tonight."

He pushed her back then and stood in her way, his faded eyes flaming angrily.

"You will listen to me! Now!" he told her hoarsely. "I'll make you listen!"

For a moment she seemed to hesitate, her dilated eyes no longer soft but filled with battle. Then she shrugged her white shoulders and went back to her chair. She did not sit but stood looking steadily at him, one hand tapping at the chair back.

"Very well," she told him. "Only let's get it over as soon as possible. I'm listening, father."

"You have some foolish prejudice against Temlock," he began a trifle weakly. "What is it?"

"Prejudice? Is it prejudice? Just because I do not wish to consider such a thing as marriage with such a man? A man who is a brawler, a rowdy, a drunkard, a thief. A murderer!"

"He is not a murderer, he —"

"He shot a man less than a dozen hours ago. Perhaps you had not heard? I learned of it as I was leaving the hall."

"Well, what if he did? I saw it. It was done in self-defense!"

"Perhaps." She didn't seem interested. "He has killed other men, hasn't he — many other men? Was it always — in self-defense?"

"In a country like this," answered Ellston hurriedly, "where men are their own judges, their own law courts —"

"You needn't go on, father. I know what you are going to say. But even if he is, as you'd prove, a very estimable gentleman, still he is not the sort of man I shall marry."

56

Suddenly Ellston's mood changed, or his mind changed. She saw in his eyes, about the corners of the thin-lipped mouth, that he was going to speak differently. She felt a quick surge of hope, hope that he had sobered a little, that he began to see the monstrosity of the thing his drunken fancy had suggested. And then, with his first words, she knew that he had merely given up one attack to switch to another.

"You owe a certain duty to your father, Marian." He was trying to inject into his utterance a certain gentleness and affection that was false, more contemptible than anything he had yet done. "I — I am in very great distress, Marian. You can help me now, you and no one else. If you fail me I am a broken, ruined, lost man."

It was cheap, theatrical. It hurt her while it disgusted her. And yet she strove to speak kindly.

"I am sorry. What is it, father?"

"Won't you sit down, Marian? Now" — when she had done as he requested — "I am going to tell you something which I have hidden from you all these years. I so wanted you to be happy, my dear —"

"Don't," she cried passionately. Oh, how it hurt, how it cut deep into a clean, proud spirit to have the man sink to a hypocrisy like this! "Tell me what you have to tell me and in as few words as you can. Don't you see I — I'm so tired —"

"I was a cashier in a bank in the East," he said, talking rapidly, eying her sharply. "A — a very large sum of money was taken — stolen, Marian. I — I didn't do the thing, of course. But it looked as though I had done it, the thief so cunningly planned his evidence. I should have been convicted on false, circumstantial evidence. I had to leave, to come away. I came here —"

"Did mother know?" she asked quickly.

"Yes. She knew. Of course she knew that I was not guilty —"

"Go on," said Marian wearily.

"That is why I have been here all these years, under a name that is not rightfully mine. If I went back, if it was learned that I am here, I should —"

"Temlock knows?" she asked, paying no heed to the rush of his words.

"Yes, yes! That is it! And unless you marry him he swears —"

When he saw her white face as she turned it full upon him, when he noted the carriage of her head as she again rose and stood very still, his words died down in his throat.

"I am sorry, father," she said steadily, although her heart pained her at every word, "that your sin has found you out. I am sorrier that I cannot help you in the way you suggest. I am sorrier yet that you should seek your way out by trying to barter to a man like Temlock your own daughter's body and happiness. I am sorrier that you should not have been man enough to take on your soul the lesser crime of killing the man who suggested the thing to you. And most of all I am sorry that I could not have known and understood, while I was a little girl, that I might have helped poor mother as one woman may help another when she understands."

And then, without looking toward him, she passed slowly to her room, opened the door and went in, closing and locking it softly behind her. And Ellston did not rise from his chair, did not put out a hand now to stop her.

CHAPTER
SIX

Scarcely had Marian's door closed behind her when she heard the board on the floor in her father's bedroom creak under a cautious but heavy tread. She knew that Ellston had not moved from his chair; she remembered now with swift indignation the creaking of the door a little while ago which had so nearly passed unnoticed.

Temlock was in the house. He had driven her father to do this thing and he had come to listen to be sure that a man whom he knew to be a coward was not a traitor to him, too.

"It is unbelievable!" breathed the girl as she stood at her little window, the fresh cool morning air blowing across her hot cheeks. "I — I didn't think he would do a thing like this!"

And yet she was not so greatly surprised as she told herself she was. Not being blind or a fool, she could not fail to know years ago, while she was still in very short dresses and very long curls, the sort of man her father was. He dressed well when she had only the old things, made over, to wear. He dined well at the restaurant when he forgot to send anything up from the grocer.

At times when there were clients and he had money, she saw little of him, and the saloons and gaming tables saw much. At other times, when there were many more creditors than clients, she saw much of him and of his weak, quarrel-some, complaining, selfish nature. If at any time in her life she should have had a reason to ask herself the question, "Would he sell me and my happiness for a handful of money?" she would have known how to answer the question.

She heard her father get up from his chair and go to his room. No sound of voices came to her, though only a thin board partition separated the two rooms. But a moment later she heard an outside door open, cautiously, heard steps leaving the house by the rear, and knew that Ellston had gone out, and that Temlock had gone with him.

It was full, bright morning now. The town which had frolicked and danced, gambled and drunk deep all night was sinking into the stupor of the sleep which follows dissipation. The saddle horses had gone from the hitching rails up and down the street; the boys who had come in from the ranges were riding sleepily homeward, dozing in their saddles, yawning over the thoughts of a day's work ahead.

Marian stood at her window a long time, looking thoughtfully out across the barren, rugged lands of the Bad Country to the west, striving desperately to solve her own destiny soberly. There was no longer any hot anger beating in her brain to make her vision clouded. A strange calm settled upon her. She looked backward over the past, she analyzed the present, she turned her eyes toward the future.

"When there is only one thing to do," she told herself at last, speaking in a low, hushed voice and with a sad, wistful little smile, "one needn't take a very long time in doing it. Only one thing left to do!"

She drew down her shade and undressed swiftly. The light little gown of blue and white with the broad sash she put away tenderly in her old trunk. Her dainty slippers and blue cotton stockings went with it. And then, her mouth and eyes determined, she dressed quickly, putting on her best riding things, blouse and skirt, her broad-brimmed hat, her boots which she laced with hasty fingers, then her gauntlets.

She went to a corner of the room and took up her violin in its case. Then, with a long last look at the little room which she had made a part of herself with its many feminine odds and ends, with best-loved books and pictures, she went out into the dining room.

She did not pause here but went on hastily to the kitchen. Hanging on the wall was her rifle. She took it down, slung it across her shoulder by its strap, ran a cartridge belt around her waist, thrust a rudely done up luncheon into her blouse and hurried out to the little stable behind the house.

A four-year-old mare, with brightening eyes and up-pricked ear, thrust a white nose out of the barn window and whickered a glad good morning.

"We're going for a long ride, you and I, Lady," the girl said softly. "We're going to play at a sort of Babes-in-the-Wood game. And so you can say good-by to West Eden. God will have to be good, very good to us, Lady."

Where were they two going, Marian and Lady? Marian didn't know; Lady didn't care. Somewhere, anywhere to be gone from here. Yes, the girl knew her father very, very well. She knew Temlock, too, a little from casual acquaintance, more from hearsay, a vast deal more from pure instinct.

She knew what would happen if she did not go and go now. Temlock would drive her father as a sheep dog drives sheep; Ellston would make her days and nights utterly wretched; he would make her life a hell on earth as he had made her mother's. She must either go away or do the thing which he commanded. Marry Temlock? She shivered.

She saddled quickly. By now Temlock and Ellston would be at the Barrel House, drinking no doubt, certainly talking about her. She must go before they came out again; go now, while the town dozed after its frolic.

She led the mare from the barn, strapped her rifle to the saddle, took her violin in her hand and mounted. There was no one in sight, not a man or woman or child. Now was the time. And where?

Her plans were formulating rapidly. She would ride west into the Bad Country. Not five hundred yards away was a gorge down into which she could ride and be lost to all eyes in Hang Town. Then she could hurry on all day, turning southward after a while, riding toward some one of the small settlements.

And then, just as she was about to touch the horse's side with her spur, a man rode around the corner of the barn and jerked his horse to a standstill not ten feet from her, sweeping off his flapping hat as he did so.

"Pete!" she said quickly.

"Yes, Miss — Pete. He un'stan.' He go 'long. Some day, bimeby, Pete he kill Temlock."

He was a half-breed, unkempt, evil looking, tattered, black with his dark blood and unshaven scraggling beard — Indian Pete who had been Ellston's servant or hired man, or what you please, for many years.

"Pete go 'long," he repeated quietly. "Pete heap savvy. Li'l w'ile ago me hear two man talk, Temlock an' your papa. Pete un'stan'. You heap mad, you go 'way. Pete go, too."

"Thank you, Pete," she said softly, a sudden rush of tears stinging her eyes. "You are very good to me. But I must go alone this time, Pete."

Indian Pete shook his head stubbornly, his ragged black hair swinging back and forth about his neck.

"No good go 'lone," he grumbled. "Too l'il girl. Pete go too." He tapped significantly the rifle under his leg. "Pete good shot," he added bluntly.

She started to argue but saw a stubbornness in the Indian's eyes which she knew no words of hers could shake. He would argue, it would take time, and she must get away before Temlock and Ellston saw her. She would let him come with her until they were far out of sight of Hang Town. Then she could send him back.

"All right, Pete,' she answered then. "Come on!"

64

She touched Lady with the suspended spur and shot from the barn toward the broken reaches of the Bad Country, followed by the Indian upon his shaggy cow pony.

Not yet had the Bad Country received its proper name upon the official maps. But the men who rode over it when they must, skirted it when they might, slipped into it for hiding and protection when they were hard driven, had always known it as the Bad Country and would always call it that until some mighty upheaval came to change its hard, almost trackless wastes.

It rose here and there into rugged knolls, flinty and barren, strewn with lava blocks and conglomerate, pricked through by thorn-tipped cactus, denizened by the unlovely desert things which need little water. It sank between the bleak hills into deep gorges, twisting like blistering, tortured serpents through a land of little shade.

It was as if an ocean in the fury of a driving storm had been held still for an instant, and during that instant petrified; it was the sort of deserted land to call to a man only when he sought to flee from his kind, a haven that protected with its very threat.

In a little while Marian Ellston with Indian Pete at her mare's heels had dropped down into the first hollow, sped around a rocky eminence and entered the tortuous gorge, which cut with its broken, upthrust fragments of rock at their horses' fetlocks. And now, if they had not already been seen, no one would see them. And it would be a keen eye that tracked here.

The girl forgot that her body was already tired, forgot that she had had no rest, no sleep all night, forgot even that Indian Pete was riding with her. The thing that claimed her eager thoughts drove out all other things now.

Behind her was a threat, a danger which made her shudder. Before her, what? That was the consideration to wrestle with. She could hide out here in the Bad Country; she would be safe from pursuit, perhaps. She must be safe from pursuit. For if they came up with her in these solitudes, those two men, one of whom she distrusted so keenly, one of whom she hated so with rising hatred, she was at her road's end.

She must not think of that, she must not let her mind dwell upon a possibility which she must make impossible! She must look beyond the Bad Country, see herself riding out of it unharmed, and shape her life anew from that time on.

Now she was alone in the world. She must make her own way. She was not afraid of that, for, in truth, she had been making her own way for years. She had given music lessons when she could get pupils; she had done little odds and ends that brought in to her the small sums of money necessary to her.

She was not afraid to work; she would go to some town and do anything. She would cook, she would strive to go on with her music, she would make up a class and teach, she might even find a vacancy in some little, sheltered country school.

Yes, she would turn south presently and ride to one of the little towns fifty or seventy-five miles distant from

Hang Town. There were range lands there; there were, too, many small farms. That would mean women and children. That would mean friends. She would build of them a bulwark between her new and her old life, between herself and pursuit.

Still she rode five miles due west before she thought of turning southward, before she remembered that she was going to send Indian Pete back. What would she do with him when she came to the settlement? What use would she have for a retainer? The absurdity of the thought made her smile a little.

"Pete!" She reined in her mare and waited for him to come to her side. "I want to talk to you, Pete."

"All right," answered the breed briefly. "Talk. Me no go back."

"But," she answered him seriously, not impatiently, as she thought how he was the only friend to care about where she went or to go with her, "I can't let you, Pete. It's so good of you and oh, I am so grateful! But don't you see, Pete, you can't help me and I wouldn't know what to do with you."

He nodded. He had dropped his reins upon his horse's neck; his dark fingers were busy rolling a cigarette. He did not trouble to look up.

"Pete un'stan'," he answered.

"That is good, Pete," she said with a little sigh of relief. She put out her hand. "Thank you. And when you get back you won't tell father —"

"No, tell nothin'," grunted Indian Pete. "No go back to Hang Town!"

"But I thought that you said —"

"Said me un'stan'," he grunted, licking the edge of his cigarette paper and searching in his vest-pocket for a match. "Un'stan' Temlock heap bad man. Him ketch you out here, then what? Then Pete not here, bad. Pete here —"

He tapped his rifle with his black nails.

"But he won't find me!" she cried, impatient now. "And I don't want you, Pete. I won't have you! Go back!"

"Um," grunted Pete noncommittally.

"I tell you," she cried imperiously, in the old way natural to her since when, a little girl, she had whipped her dark curls back and forth in displeasure of the one who had gain-said her, "I am going to have my way! I know that you are trying to be good to me but I must be the one to judge. You must let me go alone, Pete."

"Much bad men out yonder." Pete waved his arm, designating all of the mysterious solitudes of the Bad Country. "Not good you go 'lone. Pete come, too. You plenty talk, you plenty mad, no diff'rence. All same, Pete come. That's all."

And when Indian Pete took refuge in his old formula, "That's all," delivered with a fine air of finality, that ended the matter. Marian bit her lip, sat frowning at him a moment, and then giving Lady the spur, shot on down the long gorge. And Indian Pete, with a little grunt of satisfaction, followed her.

The sun climbed high through the clear, hot sky; shadows grew black at the bases of black rocks; the early breeze, which had seemed out of place here in this weary land because it had been light and fresh and singing of gay things, died down as if it had fainted and drooped from fatigue of wandering over the dry miles. The air was still now save where, yonder in the distances, it seemed a tangible, visible thing, dancing in lines of shimmering heat.

Long ago, Hang Town had been lost behind the two figures moving slowly across the burning landscape. Here in this land of lost things everything was denied to aching eyes except the scorching scrub, the glistening cactus, the scant, dry grass in the lower hollows, the blistering rocks. Since the heat of the day had sprung out upon them there had been no water.

Still this was no unknown land to Marian Ellston. She had lived always upon the rim of this menacing thing; she had since a little girl been used to riding far out alone. She knew where there was a water hole, and a little before noon she and Indian Pete rode their sweating horses to it.

Now, as she slipped from the saddle to drink and rest and eat a little, she felt for the first time that she was very, very tired. She was accustomed to long, hard rides, and yet she knew that even the hard-muscled cowboys who would be riding range today after a night of quadrilles and polkas and two-steps and schottisches would be as tired as she was. And she had but begun her journey.

Here she would turn southward or at least toward the southwest. Now she dared ride no further straight on into the Bad Country. For of the lands lying beyond this place she knew nothing; she might wander for hours, for days even, and find no more water.

Pete threw himself down upon the ground, drank deep at the side of his drinking pony, got up to squat in the shade of the solitary stunted oak by the spring, made a swift frugal meal from the package at his own saddle-strings, rolled another of his countless cigarettes, pulled his hat over his eyes and dozed. And Marian, with the bole of the tree between them, lay down and closed her own eyes. And she, too, dozed a little.

But she slept not restfully and not long. So much lay behind, so much before her toward which she must hasten, that she was anxious to be again in the saddle, to see the dull monotone of the barren earth slipping away under her mare's hoofs.

"Pete," she said when an hour had passed and she saw that the man's shifting black eyes were upon her, "I'm going on now. There is really no need of you coming with me. I shall turn south here and ride into Rocklin. It's only about twenty-five miles from here. I'll get there before it is night."

"Rocklin?" asked Pete curiously. "You know plenty folks there, Miss?"

"No," she answered a little wearily. "I know no one there, Pete. But I shall be safe. And —"

"Safe!" He grunted his interruption.

It was not Indian Pete's way to interrupt, and she looked for an explanation in his eyes. It was not his way to explain, either, and yet this time he went on to say:

"Not safe there! Why? 'Cause Pete no damn fool; he know! Listen, Miss: Same time you dance las' night,

Pete come back from Main Street. Two men talkin' in your house. Pete got good ears, got sense, hear much, talk little. Hear Temlock talk; hear Ellston. Temlock say, 'Make Marian marry me!' Ellston say, 'Maybeso can't.' Temlock say, 'Make her. Tell her she got to.' Ellston say, 'She get mad.' Temlock say, 'All right. Get mad, spunky girl, then what?' 'Run 'way,' Ellston say. 'Fine!' Temlock say. 'Run way, go some town not so far. No frien's there; me come get, night time.'"

Marian shuddered. She fancied that she could hear the men saying these things, planning upon her doing just the thing that she was doing now.

"Temlock big man," went on the Indian abruptly, after his short silence. "Bad man, thief, big man anyhow. Many frien's in Hang Town, many frien's in Rocklin, many frien's all over." Again he swept out his arm, waving widely. "You go there, pretty soon Temlock come. Then —"

He snapped his fingers.

There was truth in what Pete was saying, and she knew it. And yet . . .

"I've got to go somewhere, Pete!" she cried. "I can't stay here."

"No stay here," he answered steadily. "No go town. Pete show you. Ride li'l more longer, twenty miles over yonder." He pointed due west into the heart of the Bad Country. "Pete know water hole there, deer, rabbits, birds. Fool miner build one time dugout house. Plenty bad, good enough. Him die. You go there; you stay few day, week. Temlock can't find. No man find. No man know that place but Indian. Indian un'stan much, talk not much. Week go by; Temlock got business, go 'way; you get out, go town far off. Then you safe."

He grew suddenly silent, his eyes wandering to a distant dot in the sky where a hawk was sailing. He seemed to have lost all interest in the conversation. Marian looked at him, looked long back whence they had ridden, looked long to the southward.

And then, because she was very tired and very much more afraid of the haunts of men than of the haunts of the wild things of these bleak solitudes, she told Indian Pete to ride on, due west. And drooping wearily in the saddle, she followed him.

CHAPTER
SEVEN

It was five days and some hours after Marian Ellston and Indian Pete rode away from the spring and on into the heart of the Bad Country that another horse and rider stopped here to drink deep of the warm, alkali water and to rest a little.

They came up from the south, the lean-barreled, rangy sorrel horse and the man. The horse was sweat and gray-dust-covered, worn and thirsty. Upon its hide where the branding-iron had pressed, it carried its identification as a cow horse of the hundred-mile distant Two Bar-O. Such were the signs of fatigue upon the rangy body of an animal which nature had gone far toward building as a perfect example of tirelessness, one would have hazarded the surmise that the hundred miles had been traversed almost without time out to rest.

Behind the saddle was the man's coat, rolled neatly, tied by the leather saddle-strings, coated deep with gray dust. The rifle scabbard, strapped under the rider's leg, was empty; he carried the heavy Winchester 30-30 across the hollow of his arm. When a man carries his rifle this way in this part of the Bad Country it is an even break whether he is looking for someone or someone is looking for him.

The man's face told nothing of his purpose, gave no hint whether it were a stern quest or a wish to escape pursuit which brought him here. But he was alert; he seemed ready for anything which might spring up within range of eye or gun upon all of the wide reach of broken landscape. His eyes told that much.

The eyes were watchful, quick, unresting, as they sought into each shadow and hollow. The man's face, in spite of the quiet eagerness and alertness, was not the face of a man one might expect here in flight from justice or in that deadly search which carries men into such trackless wastes of the world.

It was the face of a young man and spoke of high good nature, of a certain sort of careless acceptance of what the day brought that was almost recklessness, of a vast satisfaction with life as it was. He might have been twenty-five; it was certain that he did not look over twenty-one.

The lines of the mouth spoke of an unbittered gentleness; the eyes, though keen, were the eyes of a boy, clear and pleasant, and, like the whole personality of him, bespoke good humor and a reckless, youthful joy of living. It was what men saw in the man's face and not what they came to read in his soul that caused them to name him "Babe" Deveril.

When he had satisfied himself with a long searching survey of the country about him that he and his horse were the sole outsiders hereabouts, he slipped from the

74

saddle and removed the heavy Spanish bit from the sorrel's mouth.

"Drink, you old son-of-gun," he said genially. "Here's hopin' you haven't forgotten the taste of water! And I'm passin' it to you straight, Dancer, there's not a cow horse born with four legs that could eat up a long trail the way you do it."

Before drinking himself he left his horse at the water hole and moved a few steps to the side, his eyes busy with something which had caught them before he dismounted and which was just now of more interest to them than water to a parched throat. There was a little damp soil half a dozen yards from the trunk of the stunted oak tree and in the soft dirt there were tracks.

"A week old," he told himself, stooping over them. "Maybe not quite that bad. Not over that. Two horses, travelin' together. Headed due west. Most likely from Hang Town. Now, who'd that be? Not Temlock, because he was in Rocklin three days ago. And anyway, he wouldn't ride north to here from Rocklin and then turn off at right angles. It might be Crag Verilees —"

He broke off, frowned at the signs a moment, found the cigarette stubs Indian Pete had thrown down and through force of habit had ground into loose earth with his boot heel. Then straightening up, looking off westward, he shook his head.

"Don't believe it. It's a little bit too good to be true. And besides, I'm missin' my bet all 'round if Verilees isn't huntin' mighty close to Temlock's side these days. They've got something on that — Mama, come and spank me! What's this?"

It was another track, lighter, smaller, fast filling with fine dust scattered by the wind. He got down on his knees to make sure, and when he had made sure he was not certain that his eyes were telling him the truth. The print was of a woman's boot! He blew a little of the loose dust out; the track though dim was plain. And in a moment he found another.

"A man and a woman!" he muttered. "Ridin' from Hang Town way, headin' straight into — that!"

Again he stared off into the west, his eyes passing over the ugly lava rock and brown soil, journeying into the dim distances where in the blue haze of the far-off landscape the rugged ugliness of the Bad Country was softened and colored to a strange mystic beauty. A woman — riding straight into — *that!*

"It might be Crag Verilees after all," he muttered, and shrugged. "Verilees and his latest love story. What a woman she'd have to be! But if a man goes down straight to hell there'll always be a woman to go with him."

Again he broke off shortly and a quick anger darkened his eyes.

"If a woman goes and mixes in the game and spoils my aim," he grunted, "I'm goin' to swear!"

But his good humor came back presently when he shrugged his shoulders again and returned to the water hole. He put his rifle down, tossed his hat to lie beside it, cooled his head by pouring many scooped-up hands of water over it and then, lying upon his stomach, drank from the little pool which Dancer had not muddied.

Neither the taste nor temperature of the water was such as would appeal to an epicure. But epicures know better than to push into the Bad Country. The water was wet and served its purpose, and Babe Deveril grunted his deep satisfaction as he squatted down to roll his cigarette.

It was already late afternoon. A hard day's ride lay behind him; at least two score of hard miles lay baking and blistering in front. He cocked his eye up at the sky, judged the time accurately and swiftly, pursed his lips as he turned his gaze to his horse, and with the first wisp of smoke curling up from the end of his cigarette got to his feet and went to drag Dancer's saddle off.

"Don't go and make any mistakes, you old wall-eyed, ugly-lookin', weak-kneed son of a sawhorse," he grunted affectionately, as he dropped the saddle to the ground and began to untie the rolled-up coat. "You're not goin' to spend a vacation here. Get out! Take your old nose out of my ear or I'll just naturally beat you to death with my fist. Yes, it's barley, you old pie-eatin' glutton. And it's the last you get — Oh, well, take it if you want it more than I do."

He went back to the oak and his own rude meal, watching Dancer with deep satisfaction as the horse thrust his nose into the little hollow where Deveril had poured his grain.

Dancer ate, his flapping lips giving audible indication of his enjoyment, blending harmoniously with the music of the crunching teeth and serving the further purpose of cleaning up the last elusive grains upon the side. His master, having eaten and smoked his cigarette, lay back, drawing his hat over his face, and went to sleep.

When he sat up again and cocked him eye at the sun he announced to Dancer that it was five o'clock and time to stagger on. He saddled, drank again, informed his horse that he was a fool if he didn't drink again himself in a second edition of hell like this, swung into the saddle and, carrying his rifle across the hollow of his left arm, rode on.

And now he was doing the thing which he had said that Temlock would not do; he was turning at right angles to the trail he had followed until now; he was following as nearly as he could the tracks which a man and a woman had made a few days ago. For it might be Crag Verilees' trail.

"A horse can do a hundred and fifty miles on a trail like this and still be good for something besides puttin' into corned-beef cans," he informed the animal under him. "We're goin' to prove it, Dancer. Now, shake a leg."

For a mile Deveril rode along a sort of ridge which led very gradually upward. Then he came to the top of a rocky hill, and, sitting there, bringing his horse to a standstill, he gazed long and searchingly in the little hollows and where the scant soil might retain brief record of a passing foot. And now, as a result of what he saw, he slipped his rifle into its case.

Here before him the land was less broken, or at least broken into less marked gorges and hills. There was little vegetation; no single clump of bushes behind which a man might be in hiding. If there was another man besides Babe Deveril within many miles of him, he knew that he should see that man long before he came within reach of a rifle shot.

Now he rode slowly, saving his horse, slumping a little forward in the saddle, dozing in the still heat of the late afternoon. At times he seemed to be asleep, his tall, clean-cut body swaying freely with the horse's stride. At times he sat straight up, his eyes clear and keen and watchful as he came to the top of a rise. At times he defied the unbroken stillness about him by breaking into a drawling, softly hummed song of the cattle lands.

So the late afternoon slipped away; dusk came and grew tremulous and fresh with the first faint breeze, whispering of the coolness of night. As from the harsh, ugly cactus in this barren land a soft, gloriously colored blossom puts forth, so from the dry, unlovely day, came the rich flower of the brilliant sunset.

Before him there was a broad and broadening band of scarlet, bordered with pure, pale shades of pink and green; even the sky above grew tinted, and far behind to the east, where again the ground began climbing upward into rugged hills and deep gorges, the blue above, the gray beneath, drew together, blended, the sky line lost, earth and air curtained with the soft-hued draperies of the evening's weaving.

The spring lay something more than twenty miles behind him now. Rest, he thought, lay at least that far in front. For he did not know of the spring of which Indian Pete had told Marian and which lay only two or three miles ahead and a little to the north of the trail he was now picking out.

"Pretty soon we won't be able to see much, Dancer," he said out of a long silence. "But then, if there should happen to be anybody about who'd like to try a little sharpshooting he won't be able —"

He didn't finish. The utter stillness of the Bad Country was broken by the clear crack of a rifle, and Babe Deveril, jerking his horse back upon its haunches, stopped and drew his own 30-30 swiftly out of its sheath.

"The son-of-a-gun —" he breathed.

And again he did not finish. There was a second shot, and he saw the streak of flame telling him whence it came not five hundred yards away, straight ahead of him, where there was a great pile of rocks.

He whipped up his rifle and fired back. There came a third shot, a scream of pain from Dancer, and Babe Deveril was on his feet, his face white and set, his eyes going black and hard.

Again he fired, running a little to the side, dropping behind a rock and firing over the top. There was little chance of his bullets finding a target but . . .

But Dancer was down, was struggling to rise and could only get halfway up to fall back again, and the rage in Babe Deveril's heart was crying for that expression which can find outlet only in hot lead. Another shot came from the pile of rocks, a bullet singing by him as it glanced from a slab of hardened lava, and then he heard the swift pounding of a horse's hoofs, running.

80

"Damn him!" choked Babe Deveril, glaring helplessly at the mound beyond which his assailant was racing into the swiftly coming night.

Babe Deveril ran forward, hoping to get to the top of the hill in time to have one glimpse of the man who had shot and run. He heard Dancer behind him, heard the horse struggling to rise, heard the strange sound of a horse moaning in pain, ran faster, came to the pile of rocks, heard running hoofs once more, clambered up and had one fleeting view of a horse and rider already growing a vague blur in the distance.

He fired, cursed when he knew that he had never had one chance in ten thousand to hit that dim, vanishing target, knew that the night had swallowed up the man whom just now he would have given his left hand to have before him, and then, his teeth set hard, he went back to his horse.

"Dancer! Poor old Dancer!"

The struggling animal grew suddenly quiet. Its eyes turned piteously, pleading upon its master. Dancer had had his leg cut once with barbed wire — that master had cared for him, and cured him. Now Dancer was begging mutely and eloquently for the almighty hand of his master to pluck out that pain which shot through his vitals, to care for him again, again to cure him. All the eloquence which a dumb brute must express in the only way which God has given to him shone in Dancer's eyes.

"Don't, Dancer! *Damn it, don't!*"

For it seemed to Babe Deveril that, more clear than the agony in the horse's eyes was his faith in his master, his certainty that the master whom he had borne all day and many days before, doing his horse's best, was going to wrench that pain out of him and make him well.

So Dancer, lying upon his side now, was very still, waiting. Babe Deveril put a gentle hand upon the neck that was outstretched toward him, and, coming close, looked for his horse's wound, looked and found that a bullet had broken the thin, tireless foreleg, that another bullet had ripped deep into the bleeding side. And Dancer was looking to him, waiting for him to quiet the pain and make him well.

"Dancer —"

Babe Deveril's voice shook on the one word and broke utterly, and the tears sprang up scalding his eyes, and overflowed and ran into his dusty face. For a little while he found never a word to say. He knew the answer he must give in the end — the only answer.

Then he went down on his knees. He put both arms about Dancer's neck and laid his soiled, tear-wet cheek against the horse's head. And so he found what to say and said it, whispering the words softly into Dancer's ear. It was just:

"Good-by!"

Of all the things in his life this was the hardest.

He turned away before the thin stream of smoke cleared.

"I'll find him soon or late, Dancer," was the thought in his heart.

Aloud he said nothing. His throat hurt him. And on foot, headed westward, he hastened on through the gathering night, his face still wet.

CHAPTER
EIGHT

He had left Dancer with the heavy silvered Spanish bit still in the horse's mouth, the saddle on its back. Dancer had done his work up to the last and it was a sort of sad satisfaction to Deveril that the faithful animal had died in the trappings which bespoke his service, and now lay in his insignia like a gentleman.

Deveril pushed on, rifle in hand, came again to the pile of rocks behind which the man who had shot Dancer had hidden, and plunged on and downward into the thickening night, praying dumbly that his good fortune might lead him the right way.

He had thought that the thud of retreating hoofs had grown faint toward the northwest and he went that way. He had no plan now, no thought but to push on with what speed he might, to follow blindly the man whom he wanted now more than he wanted Crag Verilees.

And then the swift thought came to him: "Was it by any chance Verilees himself who fired those shots?" It might be. He wished that it was, that he could be certain of it. It would be another thing to stiffen the anger within him, to steady his arm when the time came. He hoped that this, too, was Crag Verilees' work!

He had not yet thought of his own predicament. Rage stood so high in his soul that for a little as he stumbled on he did not think of himself. But the shock of realization came to him suddenly.

He was on foot; he was in a land of little water; he was without food, and he didn't in the least know where food was to be had. He knew of no single water hole nearer than the one he and Dancer had left behind them in the afternoon, and that was twenty miles away.

"He didn't even try to hit me!" muttered Deveril angrily. "He figured that if he could just kill my horse, thirst would do the rest for me. He planned me to wear myself out and go mad and die. It's very much like Crag Verilees' sort of work."

With the thought came caution. He had not brought a canteen because he would not have suffered for water if he had still had his horse between his knees. Now he would suffer. He estimated that he had some twenty miles to make on foot before he came to water, and he was already tired, already thirsty. He must push on; he must not go at that killing pace; he must not loiter; he must continue steadily.

Twenty miles! He could do it; he had to do it. It would take seven or eight hours over this broken ground; it might require ten. But he would come to the water hole of which he knew before the heat of tomorrow's sun found him out.

Still he could not, he would not yet give over all hope, vain as he knew it to be, of seeing something of the man he followed. Still he kept a little to the north of the trail which led to the spring he sought. It might mean the wasting of an hour; it might mean that, fortune with him, he would come to square accounts for Dancer before morning. Hope dies hard in men like Babe Deveril.

He stopped to make a cigarette, that old, faithful friend to the cowboy when he wants a moment of quiet thinking and thorough calm. He felt in his vest-pockets for a match and found that he had only three left.

"I sure came away half-cocked on this trip," he grunted as he lighted one of the precious matches. And then, before the little flame had died down, he swung about with a new thought and made his way back to the pile of rocks.

It was very dark. Still groping on his hands and knees he found some scant, dry weeds, a handful of twigs and a dry bunch of sagebrush. He made a little heap of his fuel close to the spot where he judged that other man had waited in hiding, and stepped away as his second match set its fire to dancing through the twigs. Here was a slim chance, but he was not going to miss a bet in this game: it was unlikely, but it was possible that the man had dropped something.

In an instant his little fire told him where the man had stood. Deveril's eager eyes saw the glint of something on the ground, wedged in between two stones. It winked at him like a diamond. Reckless of the chance that he might even now be watched, that his tall frame might make a target not impossible to a rifle ball in the night, he stepped into the circle of firelight and picked the thing up. It was an empty cartridge, one of the four that had been fired from here only a few minutes ago.

"It talks," he muttered, "but it don't say much! Winchester, and the country is full of Winchesters! Worse luck yet, it's a thirty-thirty, and thirty-thirties are as common as dirt."

He flung it away from him, his eyes again raking the ground for a sign, something that might "talk and say something!" And, because his eyes were the keen, trained eyes of the man who lives out of doors and who must, day after day, read the message written by running hoofs, he found the sign and it told him something.

He saw where the man had stood in a little clear space behind the rocks, saw the print of the boot heels in a small space of soft, dry earth. And, when his firelight leaped to its highest just before beginning to die down, he knew that the boots which had made these tracks were the same boots which had made those other tracks back yonder at the spring.

It was simple. They were old boots and, since coming as twins from the bootmaker, they had grown to have their distinct personalities. The boot on the right foot had its sole worn nearly through just under the ball of the boot and left in the imprint, otherwise smooth, a roughening in the soil. The man had stood very still here, waiting perhaps for several minutes. The tracks had sunk deep. That sign was clear.

The man who had made those boots had put into the leather a death warrant. He had made the boot for the left foot of tough leather, the other of a poorer grade.

Even the soles and heels were different. The left heel made a small, clear imprint as of a new boot. The other was broader, not so clear, and told Babe Deveril that a part of that heel was gone.

"I've got your picture, you night-bloomin' murderer," he grunted with something of satisfaction. "Just so I come up with you before you get a new pair of boots!"

His fire burned down; he found nothing more. But he had found much and he was satisfied. He stamped out the few dying embers and again turned westward, again bearing a shade toward the north.

Although, again and again, as he made his steady way, he paused and listened, he heard nowhere a sound to tell him that the man he sought was within many miles of him. The hoofbeats that had died down so rapidly came no more; the unbroken darkness gave no sign. And so he strode on, fixing his course by the stars and holding to it as well as the gorges and rocky hills would allow.

In the first hour he traveled close to three miles and though he did not know it, was close to the end of the night's journey. He was tired, hungry, thirsty. He was again in sad need of the only solace possible to him now, the solace of a cigarette. And he had only the one match left. He felt through all of his pockets systematically and carefully. He had only the one match.

"If I save it," he told himself thoughfully, "I'll be dyin' for a smoke all night. If I use it now, well, I'll know I can't have a smoke after this one and I won't know about it."

So he sat down upon a little knoll, made his cigarette slowly and lighted it. He would rest, smoke and wait for the moon which already gave a bright promise of rising. The moon came up, close to the full, and threw a mellow radiance over the hard landscape, softening it. And still he waited and rested, lighted a second cigarette from the end of the first, treasuring his fire yet a little longer.

Meanwhile his eyes went far ahead, searching to right and left for the way he should go. From the base of his knoll the land to the north swelled up in a long rise, growing steep toward its crest, promising a sort of dry valley upon the far side. Elsewhere the rough country was the same broken hard floor.

"A last slim chance," said Deveril thoughtfully. "I'll climb that ridge to the north and have a look down on the other side. He rode this way; he may have followed that hollow down there and crossed on over."

He pinched out his cigarette, got to his feet stiffly and again moved onward. It was easier going now. The moon helped him and in a little while he was making better time than he had since the start. He moved down the long slope to the base of the knoll, then climbed the longer slope to the crest of the ridge.

He stood there a moment, leaning on his rifle, looking down into the shallow valley before him. And then, suddenly, his eyes widened to a sight he had not hoped to see tonight. It was the bright steady light which *must* be a campfire a long way off, and yet which looked like the glow of a candle.

"If I'm gettin' dippy already," he grunted, "I've sure got a tough night's work cut out for me!"

For even as he looked at it the light was gone, clean gone, as if it had been what it seemed, a candle burning down there in the valley, and suddenly lost to him because it was in a house and a door had shut.

"There isn't a house in fifty miles of men and I know it!" he told himself wonderingly. "It looks like I'd better cut out loafin' and head on straight to water while I know what I'm doin'!"

And yet he waited. Still his eyes clung to the spot where they had seen the light. It was very dark down there. A clump of trees or a tall, upstanding mass of rock, he could not tell what it was, made a pool of inky blackness, shutting out the moon.

He drew a little to one side, keeping his body in the shadow of a rock there, squatting down, and still watched and waited. There came to him no sound; no further light gleamed at him to tell that he had not fancied the thing which he had thought he saw.

There was only one way to know. He must go down and find out. It was quite possible that he had seen a small campfire; that it had been built by the man who had fled before him; that the man had masked it behind a saddle blanket. If he went down he would have to step out boldly into the moonlight. There would be little hope of keeping hidden.

And yet, realizing all that, he saw every reason to go down into the valley. For a man might be there, and that man might be the man who had shot Dancer, and that man might be Crag Verilees. It was possible. And also, if there were a man there, there would be water. It was a chance and he took it.

Walking swiftly again, he made his way down the slope. He estimated that the light he had seen in the shadows was a mile away. So now he made no attempt to conceal his hastening body, stepping out where the way was easiest, until he came down to the more level land.

He made out that the spot toward which he was hastening was under a steep, bare wall of rock where flinty hills broke down sharply, and that it would be half an hour before the moon rose high enough to drive the shadows out.

It was perhaps half a mile away. He would go more slowly now, not giving the man, whoever he might be, a second chance for cowardly shooting.

He saw a deep-cut gorge running in the general direction in which he was traveling, and planned to climb down into it for the scant protection it gave him. Then he would stop after a little and again wait for the moon.

But not yet was Babe Deveril's caution sufficient to his need. It was not his way to think overmuch of the chances he was taking; it was his way to go straight after the thing he wanted.

For the second time that night the unexpected crack of a rifle broke the deep silence. For a second time Babe Deveril gave quick leaden answer, glimpsing the flash of the gun perhaps a hundred yards away from him where, as before, a man had crouched behind the rocks.

He dropped down to his knee and fired again at the spurt of flame. But he was in the moonlight; the other was in the shadow; he did not see the man at whom he fired, and the other could not fail to see him plainly. Another shot and Babe Deveril's rifle slipped from his hands and he went down on his face, a 30-30 Winchester bullet driven through his body.

The shock alone of a bullet from a 30-30 Winchester — not taking count of the tearing through flesh and bone, the spilling of a man's blood from torn blood vessels — is enough to knock a man down. Babe Deveril fell, with no brief space of time to feel pain, conscious of nothing but a blind, raging, speechless wrath. And from pain, shock and loss of blood consciousness of all things went out of him.

He did not know that a man came after a little while and looked down at him; he did not know that the same man turned him over rudely with his foot and stooped and looked into his face. He knew nothing until he saw the moon low in the west and grown silver from the sun that had not yet crept upward above the ridge of eastern hills.

He knew then that he had been lying there for all these hours, that he had lost a great deal of blood, that he was weak and sick and in racking pain, and that there was small chance of his ever riding out of this land into which he had come so recklessly.

He tried to rise, and fell back with a groan forced through his white lips. He set his teeth hard and tried again. And again he fell back.

For a time he closed his eyes and lay very still, forcing himself to think clearly, striving to remember just where it was that he had been hit. One moment he felt that he had not a drop of blood left in his body; the next he wondered if his head were full of blood, it drummed so in his ears and roared and seemed to be on the verge of bursting out. His sickness grew greater, his strength less, and he fainted.

Again consciousness returned to him. The moon was paler; it looked sick, and he fancied that it was faint like himself. The sun would come up in a little while and then it would be very hot and the heat would kill him. His throat burned and ached feverishly now. He wondered if he would die more from lack of water than because of his wound.

There came to him the strange temptation, for temptation it was to close his eyes again, to lie back and give up and die and have done with it all. And then, because he was a man hard to put down, harder to keep down, and because he had loved his horse, and because he had sworn to find Crag Verilees, he strove again to rise.

This time he located the wound, for now it pained him sorely. It was in his side, through his lower ribs. The heavy bullet had torn its way in and out, inflicting a painful flesh wound, causing injuries at which he could only guess vaguely.

He managed to grasp a rock and pull himself up against it so that he was half sitting, half lying, his back at last to the rock. He found his knife and cut his shirt away.

He slashed strips from the shirt, tied them end to end with shaking fingers and bound them tight about his body, doing what little he could to retain a little blood in his emptying blood vessels. And then, leaving his rifle where it lay because it was too heavy for him to manage now, and bringing a heavy Colt revolver from his hip and holding it before him on the ground, he began to crawl toward the spot where he had seen the light.

The sun came up and found him less than halfway. He could not stand, and the uneven ground shut out his view so that he could see only a few yards ahead of him.

He crawled a little and lay still, fearing that the heat of the sun would kill him before he could go the short distance he had determined to travel. The world swam before him and went black, the insistent drumming in his ears grew louder, his strength seeped out of him, and still he fought his way on inch by tortured inch.

More than once his weakness and pain and sickness all but overpowered him, and the temptation to the overworked wounded body to lie still and die became almost an imperative command. But still he edged on, inch by inch, like a wounded snake. He had little hope; he expected from each slight rise to look ahead and see the smoldering ashes of a last night's campfire, and nothing else. No water, no man, no horse; only a dead campfire to tell him that a man had been here last night

— and that Babe Deveril was still twenty miles from water.

Higher and higher climbed the sun, its rays warming swiftly, burning into his back now. An hour, two hours, three hours dragged on. He did not know how many times consciousness had gone out of him. He could not tell how long he lay still, his face in the dirt, his mouth rough with sand. But he remembered Dancer even when he felt his brain whirling away from him in delirium; he spoke aloud over and over, repeating a promise, and he remembered Crag Verilees.

And because he was young and his spirit was the spirit of a fighting man, because his father and mother and the life he had led had given to him a body that died hard, he came at last to a little knoll from which he could look down to the place toward which he was slowly journeying.

Long, long he fought his way up that rise which would have been imperceptible to him yesterday, lying still very often with his face sidewise, cheek down, on the rough rocky soil, too tired to care. But at last he came to the top.

He saw the low clifflike hills just before him, saw a small dugout, part stone, part log and part dirt, leaning against the cliff; saw someone standing before the little door looking toward him. He drew his hand across his dimming eyes to look again. And when he saw that it was a girl, that the sun was in her hair making soft glories of it, that she was like some radiant maiden of the dawn, he groaned and dropped his head again and gave up.

He was sure now that he had come to the end of all things for Babe Deveril. This thing was impossible, and he had gone mad from the torture of the long night and dragging morning.

Such is the way in which Babe Deveril and Marian Ellston met for the first time.

CHAPTER
NINE

Just as there are countless dim trails leading down into the black shadows of death, so are there numberless rosy paths leading back from the darkness up into the light. Babe Deveril came back when in a little more his spirit would have slipped forth from his body through the gates already swinging open for it into the vastness of the unkonwn; came back and felt life still pulsing through him, consciousness growing clear, mists dying out of his brain, hope sweetening the breath he drew painfully into his lungs.

There was much that would have been hard for him to understand, but he did not care to understand and did not try. He was content that things were as they were, quietly ready to accept them and to ask no questions.

He lay on his back, and there was a roof over him and some sort of a rough bed under him. At his side was an old rickety box that had been made into a table by the simple expedient of placing it on end and throwing a neckscarf over it. A tin can with rough edges where a knife had opened it was half filled with water, and a little spray of wild flowers made a vase of it and spoke of a woman.

His wound pained him; he touched it with shaking fingers and knew that his rude bandage was gone and that another fitting close, had taken its place. He saw a rifle in the corner of the small room and knew that it was his own. He saw that his Colt lay just by his hand on the bed.

He lay very still. It was very early morning or very late afternoon, he could not tell which. He did not care to tell which. No single bit of curiosity had come to his waking mind. His mind was too completely filled with contentment with things as they were to have in it room for anything else.

Somewhere, not very far from him, was the girl who had kept the little flickering, dying fire alive in him. He knew now that he had not been mad when he had thought he saw her standing before the dugout. But even about her and her presence here where a woman had never come before, he felt no wonderment. She would come in after a little while and he would try to thank her and she would take care of him.

In a moment she did come in. Evidently she had been standing just outside the dugout, at the door, and had heard him stir as he fingered at his bandage.

She came quickly to his bedside and stood there eagerly looking down into his upturned eyes. He saw how lovely her eyes were, how tender at this moment, how anxious and solicitous, and for the first time a little wonder crept into his brain, side by side with the contentment which had grown with sight of her — wonder that a girl so delicately, daintily lovely, should be here in a place like this.

"You are better!" she cried softly. "And you are going to live after all! Oh, thank God! I was so afraid!"

"I am goin' to live after all," he repeated weakly. "Thank God, or thank you? You have been mighty good to me —"

"Sh!" she admonished softly. "I am the doctor and head nurse and — and I believe that the thing to do is to make you lie very still and talk very little."

"Then," said Babe Deveril, and smiled up into her grave face in the way that helped gain him his name in the cattle country, "I am goin' to obey orders. But I'm goin' to thank you every single time I get the chance, all the rest of my life."

He saw that her face was pale, and he was sure that it should not harbor that pallor nor that drawn look; he saw that her eyes were tired and that there were little dark lines under them. He knew that while he had slept she had stayed awake, watching over him.

"I'm sorry I'm so much bother," he told her contritely.

"You're no bother!" she answered quickly. "You mustn't say so, you mustn't think so. I — Don't you see that I was so dreadfully lonely that I was glad to have someone here, something to do?"

"Then —" He stopped, frowned in puzzled fashion and said, "You are here all alone?"

"Yes."

"That's funny," said Babe Deveril.

He remembered now the footprints he had seen back there by the water hole — tracks made by a man and a woman. He glanced down quickly to see if she wore a boot which would have left the small, deep-heeled impression. He glanced up then, back into her eyes. There had been a man with her then. He had thought that it might have been Crag Verilees.

"You have not been alone — long?" he asked.

"No. But you are talking too much!"

"Please," he insisted. "Just a few words and I'll be good. Where is the man who was with you?"

She hesitated, and then to humor him answered:

"He has gone to White Rock for some supplies. I — I am going to stay here for a while."

That was strange, strange that she should send for supplies to stay in a place like this. But his mind went back to the thing which he must know.

"What kind of boots did he wear?" he asked abruptly.

He saw her eyes darken, saw a swift alarm in them, and understood before she could speak that she was afraid that he was going back into his delirium.

"I have let you talk all I'm going to now," she returned with an emphasis that was very positive. "You can lie still and watch me, but you must not talk unless you want something."

She left his side with the last word and went to the little fireplace he had not noted until now. She built a small fire of dry branches and bits of a dead log and dry twigs, and set a couple of tins of water close to the hearth. She was going to prepare a meal. Breakfast or supper? He began to be interested in things now. He would not ask her. Idly, feeling as in a dream, he watched her preparations and watched the slowly moving shadows by the door.

In a moment she went out to return with some fresh meat in her hands, fresh meat here in the Bad Country! He saw that it was his pocketknife which she used to cut the meat into small pieces. She was making broth, broth for him, perhaps. And so far as he could see that was all that they were going to have for — Breakfast, was it, or supper?

Then he saw that the shadows at the door were thickening; so it was late afternoon, and night was drawing near. She poked up her fire so that the room grew bright with it, and passing his bed, she smiled at him and said cheerily:

"I have a piece of candle, but we'll save that. Is there anything that you want?"

"I'd like to get up and help." He smiled back at her. "If you won't let me do that, I'd like to talk."

"You mustn't be foolish," she scolded him. "I'm going to be very dictatorial with my first patient. You are going to have some broth made out of nice young deer meat, soon. You can have a drink of water now if you want it."

She brought it to him in a small can. It was cool and sweet, and, though it had welled up through the hard crust of this desert land, there was no taste of alkali in it. She slipped her arm under his shoulder and helped him rise a very little so that he could drink.

When he had thanked her and she had again cut his expression of gratitude short, he said:

"If you won't let me talk, talk to me, won't you, please? Tell me how you got me here. Tell me all about the trouble I've been."

So as she came and went or stood by his side she told him. She had been at the door, just going for her horse to ride down into the little valley where there was shade and some water and game was to be found, when she had seen him lift his head from the ground and look at her. She was alone then, as Pete had already left for White Rock.

Pete! He wanted to ask her who Pete was, if Pete wore old boots, the heel pretty well gone from one, and if Pete carried a 30-30 Winchester. But she saw that he was going to speak, and lifting an admonitory finger against his question she went on with her monologue, so he waited until another time.

He had shocked her so when she had caught that first glimpse of him crawling toward her that for a moment she could not move, could not go to him. She saw him lift his head and then fall back fainting. She was afraid that he was dead. But in a second she knew that he was alive and that she must hasten to his assistance.

She had found him unconscious, every muscle of his body relaxed and useless, save alone the muscles of his right hand. The fingers were tight about the grip of his revolver and did not let go even when she struggled to get him to the dugout.

Yes, she did it alone. She brought water and wet his face and wrists; she washed his wound and did what she could to bandage it rightly.

It had taken a long time. She had been afraid that he would die before she could drag him that short

101

distance. But at last she had done it, at last she had managed to get him up on the bunk.

That had been Tuesday morning. It was now Wednesday evening. For two days she had watched over him, helping him make his fight against fever and delirium and weakness from loss of blood. She had fed him broth, all that she had to feed him. She had given him water, and when he had struggled to rise she had held him down. Oh, she assured him smilingly, that had not been very hard; he had been as helpless as a kitten.

"Only at first," she told him, "I was worried about your revolver. You fought so hard to keep it always in your hand. You refused to be still or to sleep if I took it away, and I was afraid that you'd shoot yourself or me in a moment of your wild delirium."

He looked to his side and saw the gun there. She laughed softly; it was the first time he had heard her laugh.

"I took it away from you and removed the cartridges," she told him. "Then I gave it back and have been quite content with it that way!"

"You don't know who shot me?" he asked.

She shook her head and he thought a look of fear came into her eyes.

"No! I was alone here; Pete had already gone to White Rock. I did not think that there was another soul within many miles of our hiding place!"

Hiding place! It slipped out unconsciously, and he was quick to note it. She was in hiding, this lovely girl with eyes filled with frankness and kindness; she and a man named Pete were in hiding!

102

From what — from whom?

Then her can of broth on the coals boiled over and she had to run to it, and Babe Deveril lay still, thinking. And in a little while she brought him his "supper" and fed it to him, making him drink it, and asking him solicitously if he could manage to take just a little more and if he missed the salt and pepper terribly.

And after he had had his broth and lay back she forbade him to say a single word, informed him that she would tell him nothing further until he had slept — and then made him want to get up and kiss her for being the sweetest, most thoughtful girl in America. For she had brought him his tobacco and papers and had lighted his cigarette for him with a burning twig from the fireplace.

"You can smoke and watch me eat." She laughed gaily then.

She had broth for herself and a venison steak which she broiled on the coals, promising him that if he were good he could have a steak himself tomorrow.

"Just one thing," he pleaded, after the first taste of smoke from his cigarette, "and I'll not say another word until you tell me I can."

"All right," she answered. "But remember, I shall keep you to your promise. And I'll promise you now that I'm not going to let you do any more talking until tomorrow morning. I'm rather afraid," doubtfully, "that I should not have given you a smoke! Now, what is it?"

"I have been out of my head so much," he said, "that I'm not sure of anything. But didn't I hear some sort of music?"

"You like music?" she asked quickly.

"Then I was right? When I got pretty well unmanageable you quieted me by singing to me?"

Without answering him she finished her own meal and put the things away, having washed the tin cans with a bucket of water and set them to dry in the square opening which served as a window. Then she came again to his bedside.

"I don't play for everybody," she told him quietly. "I am going to play for you because I know that you do like music. When you just wouldn't behave I thought about it and played for you, and you would lie still and go to sleep."

She left him and went outside.

"She's goin' out to have a couple of men bring the piano in," he muttered, staring after her. "Oh, no, I'm not off my head again!"

But she came back almost immediately, her violin cuddled under her chin, her bow in her fingers, and Babe Deveril knew that he was not delirious and that, all things-considered, even with a bullet hole drilled through him, he was a very lucky man.

"I've fired the doctor and nurse," he told her, "and have sent for the band! Let's have something lively. I feel like goin' to a dance!"

"What you are going to have," she told him as she drew the bow softly across the strings, "is going to be something soothing. And you are going — to sleep!"

He sank back on his rude pillow and listened, and his thoughts went the way she wished them to go, following the hushed, tender notes of the violin in an old, old song which men of the cattle country and men of the cities know and love. He was very tired but very content.

His wound pained him, but again and again he forgot the pain in watching the musician through his half-shut lids, in listening to the soft singing of her instrument. He tried to feel ashamed of himself for all the trouble he had caused her, and he tried to be ashamed of feeling happy with her there, playing for him. She, too, was tired, very tired. While he had slept she had watched over him. He should not let her play for him; in just another minute he should make her lie down and sleep.

And while he was thinking about it and his soul was following the tender harmonies, he forgot to smoke; his cigarette went out; his half-closed eyes closed entirely, and he went to sleep.

When again he awoke, it was pitch dark in the dugout. The fire had burned to ashes on the hearth; the moon was hidden behind a bank of clouds, or behind the cliffs. It was intensely still. He listened, staring into the darkness, and after a little heard the low sound of running water somewhere outside.

He wondered what time it was, how long he had been asleep, where the girl was sleeping. There was only the one bunk and he had deprived her of that. Perhaps she had made a bed of branches with a saddle blanket thrown over them, with a saddle for a pillow.

He found himself wondering who she was, telling himself that it was none of his business that she and a man named Pete were in hiding here, and yet asking himself over and over what sinister thing could have driven a girl like her to a place like this. He remembered the music of her violin, soft harmonious dream-stuff that had soothed him and put him to sleep, remembered the tenderness of her eyes, the low music of her voice, and no longer tried to shut out the question: "What is she doing here and who is she?"

She had saved his life for him and he knew it. But he did not know what her name was and she did not know his. For two days she had been everything to him. He thought, as his mind went the way a sick man's mind may go, that it would be happiness to be everything to a girl like her, and yet they were in all essentials still strangers to each other.

And he asked himself about Pete. Was he a husband, a brother? Was he a lover, and had their love story been in some way the reason of their flight? He was prepared not to like Pete, whoever he was! Was Pete the man who had shot him, who had killed Dancer? If not Pete, who then? And when would Pete come back?

She had emptied his revolver of its cartridges. He must see that she reloaded it for him. Suppose that when Pete came back it turned out that it had been Pete who had shot him? Then Pete would want to finish his work. He must not be utterly defenseless, unarmed as well as wounded. He must be able to defend himself and — What? Kill Pete? Kill the lover or husband or brother or friend of the girl who saved his life?

No, he could not do that. And it would not be necessary. For he began to reason calmly, to tell himself that since he knew no man named Pete it could not be

Pete who had shot him. It must be Crag Verilees or Temlock or one of the men belonging to their lawless outfit.

But anyway, he must not be unarmed again. There was still danger to him; there might be danger to her. It was possible that Crag Verilees had been here, that Verilees had shot him, and that the girl might herself be in danger from Verilees.

He grew thirsty, so thirsty that his throat burned. And yet he would not call to her, would not break the sleep which she must need as badly as he needed rest. He had seen that she was nearly worn out.

He was tempted, as the thirst raged higher and a touch of fever came with it, to slip out of bed and go outside to where he could hear the low music of running water. It was irritating him, angering him, to hear the water there and to be thirsty. And yet his moving would wake her, for she must be near, within hearing. So he lay still.

And then, remembering that she was the sort of girl he already knew her to be, he smiled, and in the darkness put out his hand to the box-table at his elbow. And he found there the can of water she had remembered to put at his side for him.

He turned to one side, lifted his shoulders a little from his pillow to drink, and saw her. For the moon had slipped through the clouds and its rays showed her to him.

She was sleeping, her slumber untroubled like a child's, and she was lying near the door, just within the dugout, not five feet from his bunk. She had thrown down a saddle and saddle blanket just as he had guessed, just as he had done himself so many, many nights out on the range, and with her head pillowed on the saddle, her blown hair about her face, her cheek cuddled into one arm, she had slipped out of the fatigue of the day into a dreamless rest.

He grew very still, leaning upon his elbows, looking down upon her. He forgot the pain of his wound, the fever of his thirst, and looked at her. The moonlight lay full across her face, and her beauty seemed to him the beauty of some dainty, fairylike dream-thing. She stirred a little and he was afraid she was going to awaken. Then the clouds shut out the moon, he heard a deep, sleepy sigh, and having drunk his water he lay back, his mind still full of her.

"She's a little thoroughbred," he told himself thoughtfully. And a little while later, his eyes frowning, he added: "I pray God it wasn't Pete who shot me — and that he's just her brother after all!"

Whereupon he, too, went to sleep again.

CHAPTER
TEN

There passed two days and nights which neither Marian Ellston nor Babe Deveril would ever forget. Strange days of solitude they were in a strange, solitary land, days made bearable to each only by the presence of the other. Deveril was a badly hurt man, and during those days the fangs of death were never far from his throat. And yet he found that in spite of the suffering which had to be his portion he was not unhappy.

He failed to see how any man, no matter what his trouble, could be utterly wretched with this girl near him day and night. And Marian, her bitterness of a few days ago by no means forgotten, her deep-cutting pain at the thing her father had sought to do, her sense of the precarious position into which circumstances had forced her, was not unhappy. She had something to do which largely shut out thoughts of her own troubles and made them seem petty to her; she forgot her own pain in lessening Babe Deveril's physical torture.

They grew to know each other far better than people usually do under ordinary circumstances in many times two days. He told her his name and she remembered that she had heard of him from Stet Davis of the Wagon Wheel. He told her something of his life in the

109

range-land to the south, something of his aims and hopes and ambitions. And she, glad for the opportunity of conversation, told him something of her own life.

They were no longer strangers. Each sensed in the other something with which he could sympathize. But Babe Deveril did not mention Crag Verilees, did not hint at the dark purpose which had brought him here, and Marian Ellston did not speak of her father or of Temlock or of her own reason for seeking the protection of so menacing a retreat as the Bad Country. A natural reserve kept each one silent upon this one point; a natural delicacy forbade any questioning upon it.

Although the girl told him her name, she did not mention the word "Ellston," for that name no longer belonged to her. She had dropped it and would have been glad if she could have forgotten it as readily. She called herself Marian Lee, as her mother had been named when a girl.

Now that she saw that her patient was not again in danger of delirium, she brought his cartridges back to him. A man had tried to kill him. She did not know who the man was or why he had fired those shots which she had heard and wondered at; but she did know that there might still be danger to him and that he had the right to be armed and ready. And many a long hour while Deveril lay on his bunk his fingers were close to the grip on his Colt, his eyes upon the narrow doorway, and he half expected to see Crag Verilees' lean, gaunt body shutting out the light, his wolfish eyes and cruel mouth sneering and triumphing and menacing.

110

"Pete should have been back before now," Marian had said more than once.

She had told him who Pete was, Indian Pete who had so long been one of her household in Hang Town, and Babe Deveril felt a deep satisfaction when he was able to feel certain that he should have no quarrel with a friend of hers, not with brother or lover or husband. And still he wondered if he had fallen from a bullet from Crag Verilees' rifle; if so, where Verilees was now, if he would come again, and if he knew of the dugout and Marian's presence here.

They lived on the meat Marian could bring into camp with her rifle. She rode two or three miles through the narrow valley to a grassy meadow, fringed with hardy timber, and there she found rabbits, quail and a few deer.

The second time she returned from her hunting she found Babe Deveril waiting for her at the door. He had slipped out of bed, managed to get his boots on, and made his slow, painful way to the threshold, where he sat leaning against the side of the door, smoking and waiting. He was very pale and she scolded him and drove him back to his bed. But after that he persuaded her that it was best for him to move about a little, that he was going to lose all of his strength if he didn't, and she gave in and allowed him to sit or lie on a blanket in the sun a large part of the day.

But when he started one evening, toward dusk, to make up his bed on the ground outside, where of late she had been sleeping, and she found him carrying her blanket to the couch, he learned that his nurse, although she had given in a little, was still boss.

"Babe Deveril," she said severely to him, "I am ashamed of you! You dare try to play a trick like that on me again and I'll pack up and go!"

And he saw that she meant it and he apologized and gave up the attempt.

"You're just a wonder girl and that's all," he told her. "I wouldn't swap you for all the doctors and nurses in the world. And," this to himself, though he felt very much like saying it to her, "if you don't look out I'm going to get myself so tangled up in love with you that it'll be plumb hopeless!"

A man like Babe Deveril, young, clean-hearted, reckless and headlong and likable; a maiden like Marian Lee, dainty and frank and gloriously lovely; days alone in a land like the Bad Country, with tremulous dawns and soft star-set dusks, with the singing of the winds and of the water behind the dugout, the singing of her violin in the old songs she loved best and he loved best; long days of infinite stillness and infinite peace; long twilights to mask that ugliness of the world and make of it a sort of dream-loveliness; long evenings filled with moon-glory and star-shine — and what is the answer? The old, old story, the "way of a man and a maid," the beginning of the endless. And the moon knew, the stars and the dawns and the dusks knew — and Babe Deveril and Marian Lee would have said that they were growing to be "real friends!"

"Tell me," he asked her once abruptly, his eyes searching and keen as they went to hers, "what sort of a place the valley is where you do your huntin'?"

"Why," she answered, seeing only a natural curiosity in his question, "it's a rather funny place to find out here. It's well watered; the hills shutting it in are higher than most of the hills in the Bad Country; there's plenty of grass and a good many live oaks and pines."

"How big is it, the whole valley?"

"We're just on the edge of it. I should say it's four, possibly five miles long. At the widest places it is something like a mile across."

"And," he paused, frowning speculatively, "there's no signs of cattle anywhere in it?"

"Yes," she answered quickly. "I meant to speak of that. I was wondering about it. Do you suppose we're near some range on the north?"

"As far as I know there's not a range within seventy-five miles to east, west or south. On the north there is the Double Diamond and the LM. They're a good hundred miles from here, or I'm off my trail. The nearest range of any kind is the Fryin' Pan, belongin' to Johnny Sanders. It's to the southeast and the handle of it runs a little way into the Bad Country. And the nearest part of that is seventy-five miles from here."

"Then," she wondered, "what cattle have pastured in here? There was a big herd there, and not longer ago than last spring."

Babe Deveril seemed to lose interest in the conversation. He drew her attention to some minor matter and from it to anything but the consideration of

113

the thing over which under all of his seeming indifference he pondered deeply all day. He wanted to be about more. He grew suddenly impatient for the return of his strength, for the time when he could walk or ride to the other end of the valley.

"It's open and shut," he told himself. "My good luck and bad have been pretty well mixed on this trip. I've found a girl that a man would be in luck to ride across a dozen Bad Countries and find; and I've found the place Temlock and Crag Verilees run their stolen stock!"

He was very sure of it. He had known for a long time that Temlock was stealing cattle boldly and on a big scale; he had known that Temlock must have some place just like this one, where men would not look for it, to pasture his stolen cattle until such time as he could rush them to the railroad or on some long drive across country. Here was such a place, an ideal, unknown place, a safe place if once a man could get the stock across the dry, intervening bad lands. And no doubt there was an easy trail somewhere with water holes to make the drive possible.

"How did Indian Pete know of it?" he asked himself suspiciously. "Is this a prospector's cabin, or is it one of Temlock's camps?"

He was anxious not to have Marian know the things which ran through his mind. If this were headquarters for Temlock and Verilees and their crowd, then it was no place of safety for her.

He already knew the girl well enough to feel positive that she was not the kind to take refuge in the fact that she was a woman, and so run off and leave him alone. He could not travel, or until Indian Pete returned and matters simplified themselves and cleared to his understanding of them, there was no reason why he should alarm her. But after she had told him of the hidden valley he was more careful than ever to have both rifle and revolver close at hand, and to go to sleep at night with his trained mind ready to wake at the first little sound.

CHAPTER
ELEVEN

A week slipped by before Indian Pete returned. During the week Marian Lee and Babe Deveril had talked through very many quiet hours and had at last told each other something of their reasons for being here. She knew at last that he was looking for Crag Verilees and for Temlock — for Verilees particularly. She did not ask why and he did not tell her. But she understood more than they put into words, and she shuddered when she thought of the thing that would happen when these two men met.

And he learned from her that it was because of Temlock that she had fled from her home and was now in the heart of the desert. She did not wish to mention her father, and she did not. So she went into no details concerning the trouble which had come to her. In some way Temlock was the cause of her fleeing from the beaten trail of men and women, and it was not hard for him to come close to an understanding.

Then one day Indian Pete, leading a pack horse, came back. It was just after noon. Marian and Babe had lunched on their broth and broiled meat, of which they were growing so heartily tired, and were in front of the dugout in the shade. It was Marian who first saw Pete and the horses.

Her glad little cry told Deveril. He turned with her and watched the Indian ride down the slope toward them. He was glad that the man had come, though he could not help a quick spurt of frowning disappointment that the days of being alone with her were gone — Suddenly his eyes grew alert, eager, as he looked at this man's boots before thinking to look at his face.

"I'm a fool," he grunted. "Goin' and comin', I'm a blamed fool!"

Indian Pete rode down the slope and to the dugout at a slow jog trot. He nodded to the girl, removed his hat, put it back and stared at Babe Deveril. In the stolid face of the Indian there was little expression, and yet a certain surprise was not gone before both Marian and Deveril saw it. Babe Deveril, looking at Pete's boots, saw that they were brand-new, not out of their box a week. Marian, looking at his face, laughed.

"I've got company you see, Pete," she called gaily. "And now give an account of yourself. Why have you been away so long? And what have you brought to eat? If you knew how horribly sick we are of meat and broth, broth and meat —"

Indian Pete grunted his answer after his own brief way and rode on around the dugout to the spring. He drank first, thirstily, and then unsaddled and watered his horses. And already Marian's quick, eager fingers were at work with the packsaddle.

"Canned things!" she announced joyously. "Tomatoes, think of that! And beans and sardines and peaches! Babe, Babe! Open it!"

She was like a child; he like a child, joining in with her in a new game. His heavy pocketknife made light of the work of ripping its rough circular way through the top of the can, and for the moment, serenely forgetful of Indian Pete, nurse and patient made merry dessert of canned peaches. They ate with their fingers or with little bits of wood sharpened and smoothed and pointed by the same knife. They got the sirup all over their hands and faces, and altogether it was a red-letter occasion, not to be forgotten.

Indian Pete watered, fed and tethered his horses a couple of hundred yards from the dugout and then came to squat near them, his black eyes taking in every movement Deveril made.

He made his cigarette and spoke briefly in answer to Marian's questions.

"Temlock, him in White Rock same time me. Him mad like hell! Think maybe I know where you are, maybe I go with you. Me —" he shrugged his shoulders after the white man's fashion — "me know Temlock got many, many eyes. Eyes in his own head like needles; eyes in Verilees' head; eyes in other men's heads scared of Temlock. Me wait one, two, t'ree day, wait for Temlock go 'way. Temlock gone, then me come back quick. That's all."

In a little while, when he had rested and drunk several times at the spring, Pete took up a saddle blanket and went to the shade of a little oak to lie down and sleep away the afternoon.

Deveril looked up from the cigarette he was making and found Marian looking at him.

"Marian," he said quietly, "you'd better tell me all 'bout this Temlock mix-up. I'm as good a friend as you've got, and you know it. If you've got-a real, active enemy in Temlock you're goin' to need all the friends you've got. You know that, too, don't you? You've done so much for me, you'll only be playin' square to give me the chance to chip in on your side. Play fair, Marian."

Then she told him, told him everything that she could without speaking of the ignoble part her own father had played. And Babe Deveril's sunburned cheeks went a dark, angry red.

"Some day," he said quietly, as Stet Davis had said before him, "Temlock will get the wrong man!"

A thing happened that afternoon that might have been delayed a long time — that might never have happened — something to alter the fates of at least three people, and which occurred that day because Marian Lee was very sad.

God meant hers to be a sunny heart and she strove to do His will and to be happy each day that He gave her. And yet hers was a small body in a big world; home had been lost to her, everyday things had been swept away, while bitterness and sorrow were planted deep in her bosom by the unthinkable thing her own father had done. It hurt her to think of him sunken to the depths

119

in which she knew he lived; it hurt her to think that her own flesh and blood was criminal, weakly criminal; it hurt her more that he lied to her than that he took bank funds which were not his own; it hurt her most of all to know how he had made her mother suffer.

These things she strove to shut out of her mind, and for the most part she succeeded. But there were times, in the stillness of night, in the hush of summer afternoon, when she could not drive them out.

Today her pain came upon her on the very heels of her light merrymaking with Babe Deveril over a tin of peaches. Some light remark, some little thing, brought her back from the froth of bantering to the lees of a real trouble; the skeleton grinned at her out of its closet, so that she grew suddenly quiet and a shadow chased the sunshine from her face.

She went into the dugout, took up her violin and with a faint smile to Deveril said that she was going off by herself to drive out her blue devils with bad music. Deveril objected that the devils would stay and she'd be draggin' all the angels out of Heaven besides to listen to her. But not even Babe Deveril's foolishness brought the smile back into her eyes.

"What for does a man want to go and make things wrong for a wonder girl like her?" Deveril muttered savagely, as he watched her walking hastily away from the dugout.

In a few moments she was lost to him where the valley narrowed and the stunted trees came trooping down to the bank of the little sluggish creek. And then because he had been awake early and had not gotten

120

his strength back yet, and because there was nothing better to do now that his nurse had left him, he went into the dugout, made himself comfortable on his blankets and prepared to take a nap.

Half an hour later he awoke suddenly from his light doze, brought rudely to consciousness by a sound so light that most men at most times would not have noted it even had they been awake. For he had grown into the habit of being always on guard, even in sleep, since he knew what the girl had to fear; since that was added to his own danger.

It was someone walking. He thought that it could not be Marian. She would not return before sunset. It must be Indian Pete. He lay quiet, listening, his eyes going swiftly to the open door.

New boots, to a man who wears his old pair until necessity and not vanity requires another pair, are apt to hurt the feet. If the man who has bought new ones has not cast away the old on a day like this, hot with blistering sun, he is apt to ease his feet by going back to the discarded footgear.

Indian Pete's boots had hurt him. As he lay on his blanket he had drawn them off to rest his feet. He had not cast away the old, but had brought them back into the Bad Country. He had them on now. Again almost before Babe Deveril saw the breed's face he saw his boots. And he raised up on his elbow, the hand at his side, ready.

He knew those boots, although he had never seen them until now, knew that the man who wore them was the man who had shot him, who had killed Dancer. For

121

the heel of the right boot was gone; the heel of the left almost as good as new.

He lay very still, watching, waiting, ready. Indian Pete was at the doorway, his tread all but noiseless. He paused there and looked in. His rifle was across his arm. His eyes were black, inscrutable, the eyes of an Indian.

"Where Miss Marian?" he asked quickly as he saw that Deveril's eyes were open.

"She's gone up the valley," Deveril answered him quietly. "I guess you saw her go, Pete."

"Me 'sleep," grunted Pete. "See nothin'."

Then for a moment neither man spoke. Babe Deveril's right hand was hidden from the Indian, lying close to his side, the steady fingers already curved tight on the grip of his gun. It was not Babe Deveril's way to seek to hide the thing he thought, to loiter on the outskirts of what was to be done. Now his eyes were frankly distrustful, and now he came straight to what was in his mind.

"What's the game you are playin,' Pete?" he asked bluntly. "You killed my horse and you damn near killed me. What's the game?"

Indian Pete's stolid face did not change. Not a muscle twitched; his eyes lost none of their fathomless blackness. His rifle, lying in the crotch of his left arm, the muzzle pointing downward and at a spot not two feet from where Deveril lay, the trigger feeling the steady touch of a finger of the right hand, did not move. He might have been an artist's conception in stone of his reserved, enigmatic race.

122

"What for you come here?" he asked suddenly.

"That, my beloved warwhoop," Deveril informed him quietly, "is none of your damn business."

For a long moment Indian Pete regarded him with thoughtful gravity. When he had spoken he had been a statue awaking to life; now he was the thing carved in stone again, not even his eyes moving as they rested upon the cowboy's, the narrowed eyelids unwinking. And then — it came with the unexpected swiftness of a flash of lightning from a black cloud — his whole being was galvanized into action.

He had leaped back so that 'even his shadow was gone from the threshold. He had in one bound sprung to the corner of the dugout and around it. Perhaps he had seen that Babe Deveril was ready, perhaps he had after all glimpsed the gun in the right hand. There came the crack of a rifle, not five paces away, and a 30-30 bullet tore its way through the little window and embedded itself in the thick log wall a scant few inches from Deveril's head.

"The son-of-a-gun!" grunted the cowboy.

He rolled over, his action as swift as the Indian's, despite the soreness of his wound, and as he moved, in the short flash of time, decided the thing for him to do — the thing which Indian Pete would not be looking for. A second bullet, crashing through the wall before the splinters scattered by the first had stopped moving, found the spot where a moment ago Deveril's body had lain. Then came a third and a fourth, fired as fast as a quick man at the trigger could work the lever. But already Babe Deveril was at the door. He sprang outside.

They met there, face to face, hardly more than room between them for Indian Pete to use his rifle. The Indian heard him and swung about to meet him, his rifle thrown up, his hand jerking down the lever, the muzzle looking the wounded man squarely between the eyes.

An infinitesimal fraction of time, one brief part of a second so short that the finest stop watch could not count it, was all that stood between Babe Deveril and death. And yet, to a man who uses his gun as swiftly, almost as naturally, as his involuntary muscles work, it was time enough. Deveril fired, fired just as the lever snapped back into place, just as the Indian's finger hardened to the trigger, fired and threw himself to the side.

He felt the pain as of a hot iron laid along his temple and knew that a quarter of an inch and a bit of immeasurable time had saved his life to him; he saw Indian Pete stand balanced a moment, saw the rifle slip from his hands, saw him settle quietly and lie still, a bullet through his brain.

"I've kept my promise, Dancer," Babe Deveril said sternly.

He drew back to the door and sat down. Suddenly he was very weak, almost fainting. He put his hand to his temple and found that it came away red. But the wound there was nothing, a scratch which two days would heal. It was not that that weakened him. It was his old wound. He had broken it open with the quick leap to the door; the blood was gushing from it as freely as when it had first been made; he was fast growing weak, weak.

And then, looking up, he saw, dim against the low sun, the form of a girl. She had come back. She was standing looking down at the quiet form of Indian Pete, looking from it to Babe Deveril, with strange eyes, eyes wide with horror.

CHAPTER
TWELVE

You have killed him!" Her voice crept through the roaring in his ears, as strange a thing as the look he saw in her eyes.

He saw her fingers go bloodlessly white as they tightened about the neck of the violin in her hand. It was a little hard for him to think clearly just then; he was thinking that her way had been hard enough with troubles aplenty as it was, and now he had killed a man who had befriended her and he had made her look upon death.

"I have tried to do all that I could for you," she went on when he did not speak. Her voice was steady and came more clearly now, and yet he was thinking that in a moment it would break pitifully and that she was going to be shaken from head to foot with passionate sobbing. "And now you have killed him — the only friend I had in all the world! Why did you do it?"

She had returned in a roundabout way, had come from the south side of the cabin and had not seen how Indian Pete had fired first. He wanted to tell her, but suddenly he felt too weak, too sick and uncertain of his voice to say anything. So he sat and stared at her until the sun behind her blinded him.

And as he sat he swayed a little and felt the hot blood against his side where it broke from the slipping bandages, and his face went white, as white as Marian Lee's face. But she did not see these things, noted nothing but the dead face of Indian Pete and the horror of it all.

"If I were a man," and her voice came to him from far, far off, "I'd kill you. It is the thing I should do, even being a woman. But one thing I can do and will do: Kill me, too, Babe Deveril and make your bloody work complete, or I shall some day send you to the gallows for this thing you have done."

He saw her move, guessed that she had gone down upon her knees at the side of Indian Pete, and then he saw nothing at all, heard nothing, knew nothing of what happened. For he had slipped a little farther sideways and the world had swum and gone black as he slipped and fell, head and shoulders across the narrow threshold, and fainted.

"I will let him die," Marian told herself in a steady, small voice which was as strange in her own ears as it had been in Babe Deveril's. "I will somehow bury Pete, poor, poor old Pete — and —"

And then she broke down, the tears came, her slender young body shook in the gust of her weeping and she lay still upon the ground near the body of the man who had accompanied her into exile.

The sun went its way lower, lower in the western sky, until it flattened like a molten ball upon the long horizon, lower still until only a glowing section of the red rim winked across the little valley, and the three figures lay so still that had a man come here now he must have thought all three dead.

Then Marian moved a little as the dusk came on, and sat up and moaned as her white face went into her cold hands.

"Is there nothing left in the world but misery and wickedness and things like this?" she moaned. "Have men gone mad and drunk on crime? And I had begun to think —"

She broke off, shivering. It was warm and close in the new dusk but she seemed chilled. Her wet eyes went to Indian Pete's face and lingered there, widening with horror, drawn to the thing she shuddered to look at. Then they went to Babe Deveril. He lay as he had fallen, and did not move. She wondered if he were dead.

"It would be only right," she told herself bitterly. "And I shall do nothing — I shall let him die!"

It was a horrible thing, but less horrible it seemed to her hot brain than to seek to keep the life in a murderer. She had not reasoned; she could not reason now. She knew only that Babe Deveril had killed Indian Pete.

It was growing dark. Suddenly the girl leaped to her feet, a new horror upon her. She could not stay here, she could not remain all night at the side of a dead man and with the man who had killed him! It would drive her mad! But she *must* stay! She could think clearly enough to know that. She could not go away and leave them like this. She must stay!

She hurried into the dugout, drawing her skirts back so that she might not touch the cowboy where he lay. She went hastily to the fireplace and with shaking fingers piled fagots and splinters of wood, building a fire. She must at least have light if even the unstable, ghostly, fancy-filled light of a campfire.

The dry, burning wood, filling the cabin with light, threw a ruddy gleam out across the two sprawling bodies. She came out again, again drawing aside so that she might not touch Babe Deveril. And she did not look at his face.

Far off she heard the shrill, shuddering, evil bark of a coyote.

She, she alone, a young girl, would have to find some way to make a grave, to bury a man. A weakness, a growing nausea not unlike Babe Deveril's, swept over her. Her taut nerves jangled. At a little sound she stared and her white face went whiter.

Then suddenly an unreasoning alarm leaped out upon her: Temlock was still looking for her! Suppose that he had followed Indian Pete after all; suppose that he came upon her now —

The firelight played fitfully over Indian Pete's still body. It seemed to her disjointed fancies that one long, quivering finger of fire pointed, wavered, pointed again. Pete lay upon his back. His arms were outflung, his open vest fell to right and left of his body. The trembling finger of her firelight touched and rested a moment upon a white, folded paper in Indian Pete's vest-pocket

In this way the thought came upon her: If she buried this man she must first look through his pockets. Indian Pete had a sister in Hang Town, a dissolute, half-breed woman with whom Marian had never spoken. But there might be something in the Indian's possession which should go to his sister. At any rate it would be her duty to see.

The fire flickered and danced, gave way to shadows and flared out again as wood fires do, and the folded paper in Indian Pete's pocket still peeped out at her. It was strangely white and clean and new to be a thing belonging to Indian Pete.

While her fancies wandered, still that fresh, unsoiled bit of paper drew them back over and over to the stern work that her fate had set before her. With a sudden gesture, half of pity, half of revolt, she stooped forward and drew it from the Indian's pocket. Moving a little closer to the open door, unfolding the paper, she read the few words in the scrawl without trouble. The trouble came in understanding what was so plain, in forcing her hot brain to conceive of a thing so inconceivable.

"God! God!" she moaned. "That You let such things be!"

Here are the words of the brief, penciled note:

Henery Lehr: Pete's did his part like he promised me and Ellston. He has got the girl safe all right. You know where. Pay him one hundred dols.

And it was signed with the one name in big, bold letters — "Temlock."

130

"Pete's did his part like he promised me and Ellston!" She read it over again to make sure that her brain had not tricked her, read it aloud in a voice which choked and which she could not make clear. "He has got the girl safe!"

The bitter chill clutching her heart grew into ice. She had never asked herself in her blind trustfulness how it happened that Indian Pete had overheard so much of Temlock's and her father's conversation. Now she knew.

For a hundred dollars he had done this thing; and Temlock might even now be riding across the desert toward her, might be a mile away, half a mile, a hundred yards away! Pete had been gone a week. He had said that it was because he was throwing Temlock off the trail. And it was because he had been looking for Temlock to tell him where she was, and to get his order on Long Henery for a hundred dollars!

She stood dazed, uncertain. She did not know what to do, where to turn. Was the world filled with trickery and deceit?

The moon, at the full now, thrust a glorious, golden rim above the low, jagged line of the eastern sky. And the moon answered her. She had watched it rise last night with Babe Deveril. She had believed in him. She had thought, "There is a man to trust, and under the manliness of him there lies the gentlemanliness!" A moment ago she had called him "murderer!" Why? Because he had killed a man?

Her brain was clearer now. She remembered that there had been other shots fired, the shots of a rifle. She had heard them first, snapping like linked firecrackers into the silence of the night. It had been Indian Pete who sought to do murder — and she had drawn her skirts away from Babe Deveril, and had left him to die — had hoped that he would die!

"God forgive me!" she gasped. "God forgive me!"

She sped back to the door. She went down on her knees there, her white hand flying to Deveril's face, seeking the wound that had stretched him out so still and pallid. It was not burial of the dead which she must look forward to tonight, it was care of the living.

She saw the streak of blood across his temple and her heart stopped beating as she thought that already he was dead. But in a breathless moment of bending low over him, so low that her hair and his met, she saw that there was only a scratch which had nearly ceased bleeding.

It was the old wound. A short search told her that. She drew him in a little farther across the threshold, shut the door, forgetting the man lying outside, threw a blanket to the floor and got Babe Deveril's head and shoulders on it. And then, her fingers steady at last and very, very gentle, she again cut at his clothing with his own knife and laid bare the red wound in the white side.

She bathed it, bandaged it once more, bathed his head and wrists and in a little while drew him back to consciousness.

His eyes flew open and regarded her searchingly.

"I had to do it, Marian," he whispered "I'm sorry —"

"Sh!" she commanded very softly. "Lie very still — and get well, Babe Deveril. I need a friend, oh, more than you know! I need you to get well!"

There is one thing which will shorten the longest night, soften the hardest blow that fate knows how to deal, one thing, which Pandora let flutter out of the golden box and whose wings have never grown less rosy and radiant than when the fair mischiefmaker turned away ills and one great bood loose to roam the world — just Hope. Hope, soaring high in Marian Lee's heart that Babe Deveril was going to get well, that he was going to be the friend her destiny called for, that he and she were going to ride free of the shadows and mystery and threat of the Bad Country; hope in Babe Deveril's heart that one day she was going to care as he knew he already cared.

Morning broke and Temlock had not come. Then and then only she told Babe Deveril of what she had found in Indian Pete's pocket. And when she asked him for it he gave an account of how he had been attacked by Indian Pete. He told her, too, of the boots, of the death of Dancer and of his certainty that it had been a bullet from Pete's rifle that had stricken him that other time.

"And you did not know each other?" she asked wonderingly. "Then why should he have shot you?"

Babe Deveril's face hardened.

"He was one of Temlock's men; one of Crag Verilees' men," he answered sternly. "He would have made another hundred dollars, perhaps!"

"Tell me," she said, for now she could no longer keep from her lips the question that had so long been upon the tip of her tongue, "why are you looking for Crag Verilees?"

Deveril was sitting propped up against the wall, looking out across the valley that was filling with sunlight. She saw his lips close tight, saw something in his eyes that drove a quick, unreasoning fear into her. The hand at his side tightened.

"It's not a pretty thing to talk about, Marian," he answered her slowly. "And talkin' about it can't help much. I've just got to keep on lookin' for him until I find him. And then —"

"And then?" she insisted.

"Then," he said sternly, "it's goin' to be nothin' new much. Just man and man, and quick, straight shootin'."

"Oh!" she cried hotly. "Why do you men do these things? If Crag Verilees has done something, he should be punished for it; if he has committed crime on top of crime, then why not seek that redress which all men may have? Why don't you call in the law?"

"The law?" He interrupted her there, and she saw that a fierce light burned in his eyes which she had never before seen in any man's eyes. "The law? There is no law here, Marian, no law which is tireless and sleepless, which will bring a man like Crag Verilees to justice, except what men who live hard and die hard call the red law — the law of a man's right hand, the law there is no bribin'. And now" — his old smile came back into his eyes — "let's forget it and have some coffee."

That day Marian Lee and Babe Deveril buried Indian Pete. Babe's strength came back to him wonderfully, or at least he succeeded in convincing the girl that it did. For he had made up his mind to get this thing over with and he wanted to spare her all he could.

Then they were to get out of this hidden valley. For already Temlock knew that the girl was here, and Temlock might even now be riding toward them. And he could not tell whether Temlock would be riding alone or whether he would have a dozen of his crowd at his back. And the danger was not Babe Deveril's danger, it was hers. He could delay his meeting with Crag Verilees; it would keep. But he must not delay the time of her departure.

When she would not listen to his plan he strengthened his argument by saying simply:

"We've got to do it. It won't kill me to ride seventy-five miles. We'll make it to Johnny Sanders' place in two days. If we stayed here what chance would I have, hurt like this, against the gang that travels with Temlock?"

And when he told her what he had guessed, that this was the place where Temlock and Verilees hid stolen cattle, that at any time they might appear, driving a stolen herd, she accepted his plan, half reluctant, half eager. And that same day, Marian upon her mare, Lady, Babe riding Indian Pete's mustang and leading the pack horse, they left the valley and headed south across the Bad Country.

"We're goin' to get to Johnny Sanders' place in two days," he had told her. And to himself he had said, as

135

he turned slowly in the saddle and looked back upon the dugout where he had suffered so much pain and found so many happy hours: "I'm goin' to get well real soon. And then — then I'm comin' back. Because now I know where to find Temlock — and Crag Verilees!"

CHAPTER
THIRTEEN

They made a late start and traveled slowly through the heat, leading Indian Pete's pack horse which carried their all too few belongings. Babe Deveril pointed out the way they would go, almost due south; he called her frowning attention to a far blue line of hills that he said were a good forty miles away. She believed him; she could hardly see them, a vague, bluish, irregular and wavering line against the washed-out blue of the horizon. But finally she did make out a tiny V-shaped notch in the pale blue hills.

"That's Coyote Pass," he told her. "We head straight for it. As far as I know there's no water until we get to the pass; there's a good spring there comin' out of a cut in the hillside, nice and cool, runnin' out under red willows and some big ferns. That's camp for tonight, late tonight, if you feel like the forty-mile ride."

"I can't get away from this place fast enough, far enough!" she exclaimed feverishly. "Let's hurry — Oh! Forgive me, Babe Deveril! I'm so selfish! It must be agony for you to ride at all!"

"I'm all right," he told her lightly. "You patched me up in great shape. It's only, with a long hot ride ahead of us, that it pays to let the horses take it easy. They'll be gettin' thirsty before long."

He and she had provided theselves with water, filling Indian Pete's canteen; and they had brought along the tinned goods that Pete had added to their slender larder, goods selected by one who knew these dry lands and their patient way of killing human invaders of their solitudes who were not thoroughly versed in their intricate methods of homicide. At first the girl had wondered, for one thing, at so many cans of tomatoes! Before long she saw the reason; in them you had both food and drink.

Miles ahead and hours away, in their snail-like approach, was a monstrosity which lifted itself like a black tower into the cobalt sky. The girl wanted to ask what it was, but did not through sheer listlessness and weariness; she wondered bleakly if ever again her body would feel young and zestful and athrob with eagerness, if ever again she would leap out of bed and run to a window to breathe deep at the million-year-old, ever-new glory of sunrise — if she'd ever dance again as she had danced just the other night, her heart on her sleeve and her life in her heels! She said to herself dismally, "I guess now I know how it feels to be old, terribly old!"

They drifted along endlessly, across ragged, broken flats, through fields of lava rock, along little, mysterious paths through tecolote and ugly thistles and scant, dwarfed, dry brush and vicious cactus, and the sun set the hot air quivering visibly, and a draught of tepid water out of the canteen was heavenly.

138

"Our poor horses!" said Marian.

Babe Deveril dismounted. Before they had left camp he had scouted around for the various tin cans they had punctured or cut half open with his knife; he had brimmed every tin with water, had stuffed up the holes as best he could, and had slung the cans with a bit of thong behind the bundle the pack horse carried. He got out a frying pan and poured some of this water into it; he let each horse stick its nose down into the life-giving liquid; he washed the worst of the dust out of their nostrils; he made sure that each beast of them had anyhow a cupful of water, good wet water, to dribble down its throat.

They rode on, straight toward that towering monstrosity, still so far ahead, cleaving the southern sky.

"He's good," said Marian Lee, gently patting her horse's shoulder. "If he hadn't been, he wouldn't have thought about you. I didn't. You thank Babe Deveril. He is a strange man, isn't he? But he is good to us!"

"You're a funny girl," said Babe Deveril, and she started and for an instant experienced a sort of guilty feeling. He had been picking her brains, that's what he had been doing. Saying, like that, "You're a funny girl!" When she had just confided in her horse —

"What do you mean, I'm a funny girl?" she demanded.

He chuckled softly.

"I just got to thinkin'. Here I've known you I don't know how long. Some of the days and nights have sort of telescoped for me; they don't all of 'em seem quite real when I try to look back on 'em. You saved my bacon, and there's no misdoubtin' that. And we've had a few scraps of talks. But, like I just got to thinkin', you haven't said a dozen words about yourself, what you're doin' way out here and all that. You don't want to talk about it to anyone, is that it? Or you don't trust me yet?"

She hesitated. Then:

"I do trust you, Babe Deveril! You say I have saved *your* bacon! In what sort of a pickle would I be but for you!"

"You mean Indian Pete and Temlock?"

She nodded. "Let's hurry on," she said. "Oh, let's hurry all we can!"

It was almost dusk when they came to that odd looking, ragged column thrusting up into the sky. An hour or two before they reached it she made out clearly what it was, one of those incongruous freaks which nature at times loves to erect from the floor of broken flat lands like these, a great tower of rock, a single weathered and eroded shaft thrusting upward to a dizzy height. Low as was the sun, the heat was still stifling; there would come no real coolness until the reddening sun went down. But the spire of rock cast a pleasant black shadow; she thought of the great rock in a weary land. The horses hastened into the shade; the girl and Babe Deveril came down out of their saddles with but the one thought of taking prompt advantage of the luxury of shade. She sat with her back to the base of the monolith; he sprawled, loose-muscled, a yard away.

140

They had a glorious, deep drink of water. "Was there ever anything as good as water!" The answer, had you asked them, was a positive, "No! Never on earth!"

Babe Deveril, lazy on his back, his eyes low-lidded as though he were half asleep yet their gaze on her most of the time, told her about the lofty spire of rock affording them their late afternoon shade.

"Signal Rock, folks call it mostly, though there are some that just call it Indian Rock. Used to be a lot of Indians all spread across the Bad Country, in the hills mostly on the rim of the level lands. Indians clean from the hidden valley we just left all the way to here and on into the little hills we're headed for. Way up on top of this rock we're usin' for our parasol there's a flat place big enough to stand on without fallin' off. They used to light fires and send up smokes from up there, doin' their telegraphin' that way."

"Mercy!" she exclaimed, and craned her neck to stare up at the dizzy pinnacle. "Do you mean that they could climb up there?"

"I've been up." He nodded. "It's not so hard if you know just where to tackle it. There's one place where you crawl up a sort of split in the rock for twenty feet or so from the ground; from there on there's a crooked sort of ledge a couple feet wide, then some crazy steps that they chopped into the rock, then another long slantin' crack that's pretty easy goin', then some more steps and you're on top. Like to try it? You can see half around the world from up there."

For answer she gave him a vehement, almost explosive, "No, thank you!" He chuckled again, and for

141

a little while she thought that he had dropped off into a comfortable doze. Hardly flattering to her, yet oddly companionable, cozy even! And then she caught the glint of his eyes through the nearly shut lids; he was looking at her and the slightest, shadowy twitch of his lips made her think that he was amused.

She pretended not to notice; she closed her own eyes and rested and, for her part, did actually doze off.

She awoke with a start. She was alone; she didn't see him anywhere. She jumped up, calling: "Babe! Babe Deveril!"

His voice floated down to her from high above. She moved backward from the base of Signal Rock until at last she could see its crest; then she saw him standing on the very top, his body a black figure against a saffron sky. The sun was down; the night breeze was blowing soft and cool; she could see the rag of his torn sleeve fluttering merrily.

Seeing him poised like that, way up there, made her flutter — "like his torn sleeve!" she thought. "Like a rag in the wind!" He seemed so insecure at that dizzy height, like a man poised atop a flagpole! As though a puff of wind might sweep him off, send him hurtling down —

"Come down!" she called. "It's almost dark — we'd better be on our way again."

"Up here it's still daylight," he called down to her. "Won't you come up? It's not dangerous. Bring the rope from my saddle; I'll come halfway down to meet you; with the rope around you I'll climb up ahead again. Once you're up here, lookin' the world over, pickin' out the part of it you like best, you'll be glad you came! Kick off your boots first."

What made her yield she did not know. For one thing she was rested now, she wasn't afraid as she had been, and on top of that he assured her she could do it without danger. And to stand up there in the sky as he was doing — to stand there with him, looking the world over —

"Coming!" she called, and got the rope and kicked off her boots.

He met her more than halfway down. He showed her just where and how to start the climb; he put a noose of the rope about her, then climbed on ahead, going slowly, keeping the rope taut all the while. That taut rope gave her all the feeling of security in the world!

And at last they stood together upon a fairly flat surface at the top of the tower of rock, a place some ten feet across with a few ragged shafts of stone like monstrous broken fangs standing up along its rim. She crept close to him; to steady her and make her secure he put one arm about her. The wind freshened at every moment; it set her hair flying, whipping it across her face, stinging his cheeks with its snapping curls.

"It's lovely!" she gasped. "Lovely beyond words!"

"You should see it on a moonlight night!"

Already the first low-hung stars were out. The Bad Country was softened indescribably, with amethystine, gauzy colorings in its gorges and clefts, and the far hills about the hidden valley were like melting cloud shapes, darkening and flattening down. Ahead were those other

143

little hills toward which they traveled, and she saw clearly Coyote Pass, with a big star like a lamp lighting the way hanging low over it. Beyond the hills she saw vaguely a space of wide, billowing level lands.

"That's the handle of the Fryin' Pan ranch," Deveril told her. "Johnny Sanders' place that we're headed for. See way over yonder what looks like somebody's spilled a bucket of quicksilver? That's runnin' water, that's what that is! Big Little Creek, they call it, headed down into Johnny's cattle country."

She drew a deep, deep breath. The air was sweet, fresh, cool — clean! The world was a lovely place! She didn't feel old any more; she didn't know that she was smiling, but she was. That was because she was remembering how she had wondered if ever again she could thrill to a sunrise, to anything! Up here she was already forgetting so much of the horror of these last few days, of Indian Pete and Temlock —

"We had better go, hadn't we?" she said out of a hushed silence.

"Yes. First, what I came up here for. I had a hunch I'd find something like this. Look."

At their feet — at first she couldn't make out clearly what it was — was a black heap of something or other. She stooped and saw that there had been a fire here not so very long ago, certainly not as long ago as the time when the Indians used this as their signal tower.

"Signs of Temlock and Crag Verilees, is my bet," said Babe Deveril. "There's times, I guess, when they're drivin' stolen stock over to their valley and they want to give one another the all-clear sign or send a warnin'.

144

Signal Rock's the place for that sort of thing, carryin' on the same way it's been done hundreds of years. And —"

"Oh, let's go!" Marian said hastily. "It's getting cold up here in this wind!"

Each one of their horses had about two cupfuls of water before they started. "We'll have water aplenty pretty pronto now," said Babe Deveril. "Even enough to wash in! Just think of that, young lady!" She did think of it! "And if you feel like it," he chuckled as they headed on south, "while I'm stakin' the horses out tonight, you can even take a plunge! There's a pool in the canyon bigger'n a queen's bathtub. Fun just to splash water, waste water, throw it away, huh?"

She looked up at the stars which were now rushing out into the sky. She thought: "Stars! A cool wind blowing! High places! And water! Water to splash in, to waste!"

High places! The very pinnacle of Signal Rock! With the first stars, with the little night wind in her uplifted face, in her hair! With Babe Deveril's arm around her —

When at last they rode into the narrow gap through the hills — a steep-walled canyon it was, Coyote Pass — all that she knew was that she was fearfully tired. She could scarcely slip down from her saddle through weariness. How long a mile could be, and when you added mile to mile to endless mile you just went along as in a dream, drifting, your own volition fast asleep, letting yourself lie without purpose in the arms of circumstance.

But she sprang up! There was Babe Deveril, sorely handicapped by his old wound and the new one, unsaddling, opening the bedroll, taking care of the horses!

She watched him but didn't say anything. He vanished in the dark with the horses plodding after him. She made a small bright fire; she washed the frying pan at the spring; she dug hurriedly through their small larder. He would be hungry. As for her, at the moment she did not think that she ever wanted to look at food again; she craved only to drink once more of that purling, laughing, cool, cool water, and to curl up and go to sleep!

He came back with a huge armful of leafy willow branches and broad ferns; he piled them high in a sheltered place, well back from the trail, for her, where there was a deep indentation in the rocky wall of the ravine. He spread his canvas over it.

He made a bed to dream on!

He called cheerily to her, "I never smelled such a good supper in all my born days!"

A little warm glow came to her that was like the last flush in the sunset sky. She called back to him, though she could hardly see him through the dancing shadows, "I never saw such a bed in all my born nights!"

And they laughed together.

"I'll tell you something!" sang out Babe Deveril through the dark from his own sleeping place, a score of paces away, just around the abrupt turn in the trail.

146

"Yes?" she answered sleepily.

"Like it here, overnight?"

"It's lovely! After that awful day in the Bad Country, it's like a dream come true!"

"Good girl! Well, listen! I know a place — I've had my eye on it for four-five years. It's a little valley, oh maybe ten miles long and two-three miles wide, and there are high mountains, purple-colored early in the mornin' and when the sun's slantin' down and it's gettin' on toward twilight, and there's more green grass than you can poke a stick at — and runnin' water! Water runnin' wide and free! And there's even a place where the water comes throwin' itself away in a waterfall down the mountainside that when the sun is right or you see it under the full moon, is all shot full of rainbows! Maybe someday —

"It sounds like heaven," she called back softly.

"Maybe? Someday?"

"You've been good to me, Babe Deveril!"

"Good night," he called back. She thought he sounded young and rested, all made whole again, brimming with lusty youth.

"'Night," she called back, and snuggled deep down into the nest he had made for her.

CHAPTER
FOURTEEN

Fifteen minutes after they rode into the Sanders corrals, Marian Lee felt that she was in her own home where she had been born, raised and loved. For Mary Sanders, whom the boys from ranges many miles distant never thought of calling anything but "Mother Mary," took the girl into her round arms and into her heart at the same enveloping moment.

"You poor little motherless thing!" she cried softly. "You just come to Mother Mary an' the very first wicked man as shows his face aroun' the ranch to pester you is goin' to get it slapped clean off'n him."

It had been late in the afternoon when Babe Deveril and Marian Lee had come to the Frying Pan outfit. Johnny Sanders himself, a little wizened brown man whose hair was beginning to thin on top and turn gray at the ends, was at the stable and saw them coming. He came down to the corrals to meet them, and the girl who had heard much of Johnny Sanders from Deveril felt a quick disappointment in the man. His face was hard. There was something in his eyes that spoke of sternness and relentlessness, bitter eyes and a bit menacing.

"Hello, Babe," he said colorlessly. "Get down and throw your stock in the barn."

He did not touch his hat to her; he did not seem to have seen her. He did not put out his hand to Deveril. He chewed at a fresh straw and gazed with thoughtful keenness at the cowboy's white face.

"Hello, Johnny," Babe Deveril returned with a trifle more cordiality. "We're stayin' a day or so if you don't care. This is Miss Lee."

"Howdy," said Sanders in the same indifferent voice.

The sound of voices brought Mary Sanders hurrying out of the house and down to them. But before she had dried her hands upon her apron a man had heard, too, and came with swift long strides out of the barn. He stopped dead in his tracks when he saw who it was. A quick light of pleasure shot up into his eyes and his face reddened a little under the tan.

"Why, it's Stet Davis!" cried Marian joyously.

She slipped from the saddle and put out her two hands to be engulfed immediately and heartily in Stet Davis'.

"Hello, Babe," Stet answered, his face still hotly flushed. He had surrendered Marian to Mary Sanders who pushed him aside and took motherly care of her from that moment. "You're quite some ways off'n the Two Bar-O."

"Not much further than you're off of the Wagon Wheel," laughed Babe Deveril.

He, too, slipped from the saddle, and, now taking a step toward Stet Davis, put his hand out. But he swayed a little and his white face grew whiter, and he

149

stepped back unsteadily and clutched at his horse's mane.

"What's the matter, Babe?" Stet cried sharply. "Hurt?

Deveril nodded. Stet came to him quickly and ran his arm about the other's body, walking with him across the corral to a box upon which Deveril dropped weakly. Johnny Sanders, chewing quickly and hard at his straw, followed and stood looking down at him, waiting for the answer.

"You look like you'd been drawed through a tight knot-hole an' hammered back again," he grunted. And then lifting his voice sharply he shouted: "Mary! Get some coffee on an' see if I got a shot of whisky left. Babe's shot up. I reckon."

"Run acrost Crag Verilees?" asked Stet Davis quickly.

"No. But one of his crowd, a breed called Indian Pete. Give me the makin's, Stet. I'm clean out."

Stet produced the tobacco and papers, his eyes frowning solicitously as they rested on the Two Bar-O man's drawn face. Johnny Sanders gazed at Babe a moment in silence, grunted and led the three horses into the barn.

"Herd Babe on up to the house," he called back to Stet over his shoulder. "Sling a jolt of whisky in him an' keep the fire goin' for coffee. I'll be up in a minute."

"Injun Pete?" demanded Stet incredulously. "You mean he's one of the Temlock-Verilees bunch?"

"He — was!" Babe assured him calmly as he rested and drew gratefully at his cigarette.

150

"You ol' son-of-a-gun!" Stet cried joyously. "I always knowed he was crazy as a Injun oughta be, but I never guessed he had gumption enough to go stirrin' you up! Tell me about it."

So Johnny Sanders watered and fed the horses he had unsaddled and came out of the barn; Mary Sanders and Marian Lee went to the house and got into each other's way getting the coffee on, and still Deveril and Davis were at the corral talking. For, when Babe had told his story as briefly as he knew how, Davis had his own to tell.

Word had got about that Marian Ellston had disappeared from Hang Town on the night of the dance. It had been three or four days before anyone worried, because Ellston had answered questions put to him and had said that his daughter had gone to Rocklin to visit friends.

But when Stet Davis had heard that she was gone, a quick fear that all was not right with her leaped into his mind. He had had the last dance with her; he had taken her home and she had said nothing about a trip. That was one thing. Another was that she had promised to let him call to see her, and he knew that it was not her way to do a thing like that. He had come into Hang Town as fast as a horse could carry him and lost no time in finding Ellston.

Ellston had said again that she was in Rocklin. Stet Davis had looked him straight in the eye and had made him say it over again. He asked him bluntly the name of the people with whom she was staying. Ellston gave the name of Larkins, and Stet Davis knew that Marian did not know them at all, for he had once mentioned them to her and she had surprised him by asking who they were.

This had been enough to set Stet Davis riding day and night on her trail. He knew that her father was a "little crook," and that he was "as thick as horse thieves with Temlock." He was worried. He had threatened Ellston and then had regretted the threat as soon as the first heat of his rage had cooled. For he had gained nothing and had let Ellston know that he was on the lookout for a crooked deal of some kind.

But he had forced his way into Ellston's house, driving the man ahead of him with a threatening forty-five and had found that Marian's violin was gone. That brought him his first surge of hope for her; she had had time to take that with her and had taken her rifle, too. And Lady was missing from the stable.

Marian had ridden away, perhaps alone. But why? Had something happened just after she had left the dance, just after he had told her good morning? He couldn't explain it; he could only ride from one end of the country to the other, looking for her or for some sign of her passing. He had ridden to Rocklin and had drifted this way to the Frying Pan. He had never thought of her riding straight into the Bad Country.

"When I first saw you two," Stet ended a bit sheepishly, "my first bet was I was a fool all along an' she'd run off an' got married to you! An' then," with a deep breath, "I knowed better!"

152

For a moment the two men looked into each other's eyes searchingly. And then both men dropped their eyes to their cigarettes.

They were very silent as they went with Johnny Sanders to the house.

But they could not long remain silent in Mother Mary's kitchen. She was not the merry-hearted little woman to tolerate so sinister a thing as silence in her domain. She clattered away as she poked the fire and looked at the coffee and brought the whisky bottle. She scolded Babe Deveril for getting shot, Marian for not having come to her long years ago, Stet for sitting on the wood box when she wanted to get a piece of wood, and Johnny for not having reminded her to fill the lamp.

And they all brightened and warmed under her scoldings and obeyed her meekly in all things and loved her for being a chatter-box on the surface and a sweet, soft-hearted woman under it all. Marian felt a quick suspicion that even hard-eyed little Johnny Sanders loved her and had to struggle hard to conceal his constant wonder and admiration for the woman who had consented some twenty odd years ago to accept his name.

"Injuns is just like grasshoppers," announced Mother Mary, bringing her flushed face up from an investigation of the mysteries of a piping hot oven. "Good Goddlemighty can't tell which way they're goin' to jump next. Stet Davis, ain't you got no nose? Can't you smell them steaks beginnin' to burn, an' you settin'

153

right square on top of the stove! Johnny Sanders, ain't there no place for you to stan' in but you got to plant them hoofs of yourn plumb center in the middle of the floor an' make me chase aroun' you every time like I was dancin' aroun' a Maypole!

"Babe Deveril, you set still! If I want a bucket of water I can pick it up without you gettin' in the way, can't I? Hmf! You men folks — Miss Marian, if the time ever comes when you think of marryin' some fool man, you jus' come tell Mother Mary. I'd so dratted soon make the brute a pie with squirrel pizen inside he'd — Johnny, give Babe there a little sip more of whisky. He looks whiter'n a sheet. Folks would say you was savin' it for yourse'f! Marian, you just leave that table alone! Johnny'll give me a han'. He's just gettin' in the way anyhow —"

And so it went, with Mother Mary like a whirlwind for activity and monologue, until the supper was ready and the oven had disgorged its crisp, brown secrets. And then the supper itself on the long table in the dining room, where Mother Mary presided over the coffeepot and dessert, leaving the distribution of the thick steaks to Johnny's brown hands, but superintending even that duty as she commanded him not to expect a young girl like Marian or a boy like Babe Deveril with a bullet hole through him to enjoy a piece of sole leather. Mostly, tonight, her mother heart, warm always and big and tender, went out to the girl who was motherless.

"I ain't worryin' about you, Babe Deveril," she told him severely. "You're just like the rest of 'em, rampsin'

154

aroun' lookin' for trouble. Gettin' shot up once in a while does you fellers good."

But when it came to the pie — and there one might judge Mother Mary much more correctly than by the things she said — the brownest, most succulent bit went to Babe Deveril, and she contented herself by giving Marian the "secon' best."

And two or three times, when she got up hurriedly and went quickly to the kitchen upon some errand not clear to those at table, she merely went behind the door and dabbed at her eyes with the hem of her apron. For the mother heart was a hungry heart — when there were many at table she always missed the absent one the more — and when she mothered other women's boys and girls she longed so to mother her own.

"Where's Charlie, Johnny?" Babe Deveril asked early in the meal. "I haven't seen him for quite a while."

Johnny Sanders' stern face grew sterner and his mouth hardened. But before he could answer Mary Sanders spoke for him, a bit hurriedly.

"Just rampsin' roun' like all young boys," she said bravely. "He's up to the Arrow now, punchin' with Emmet Wood. He — he'll show up tomorrow, I reckon."

Johnny Sanders looked at her sharply.

"What are you talkin' about Mary?" he demanded roughly. "You don't know when you'll see hide or hair of the boy. He —"

"You shet right up, Johnny Sanders!" she fired back at him, her face flushed. "I say Charlie'll show up tomorrow! An' I know, don't I, bein' his mother? You men make me sick! You're always throwin' it into a boy if he cuts loose an' runs kinda wild for a spell. You done it, didn't you, before a woman with some gumption got ahold of you an' toned you down a bit! An' I reckon Babe here an' Stet has hit the high places more'n once an' they got both feet on the groun' now, ain't they? You just leave Charlie alone!"

But Johnny Sanders' eyes and mouth remained hard and skeptical.

"I didn't know you'd heard from him, that's all," he said shortly.

"I ain't heard from him!" she retorted. "Stet! Can't you see you're jabbin' that pore girl clean off'n her chair with your elbow?" Stet grew red and lowered the elbow in question and moved his chair an inch or two, and Mother Mary went on: "But even if I ain't heard from him, I know he'll be home just the same. Yes, if he has to ride across a dozen Bad Countries, or walk for that matter, with a broken leg. I guess you've forgotten something, Johnny!"

Whereupon Johnny Sanders looked at her steadily a moment, then questioningly. Then his eyes went swiftly to the calendar on the wall and he grew suddenly and deeply and redly embarrassed.

"I'd forgot, Mary," he said rather gently for him. "I kinda lost track of time."

Both Deveril and Stet Davis looked frankly curious; Marian sought to conceal the curiosity which was as strong in her.

Mother Mary answered the unspoken question briefly and simply.

156

"Tomorrow's my birthday," she announced a bit defiantly. "An' Charlie —"

But again she broke off to hurry to the kitchen, to disappear behind the door and to remain just a little longer than before. For fate that had been hard enough for Mary Sanders in many, many ways did not forget to be kind in one way that was big to her, and never yet had her boy forgotten to ride home for her birthday.

She had not seen Charlie for a year; she had not heard from him once during that time. But since evil news flies fast, she had heard of him; and even her mother's heart which defended her boy stanchly knew that the things which she had heard were true. And yet tomorrow was her birthday, and the pies she would bake the first thing in the morning Charlie would eat in the afternoon. She clung to that with a sort of grim desperation.

When Mary Sanders came back from the kitchen, Babe Deveril had switched the conversation into a new channel by asking Stet Davis about the Wagon Wheel, the stock they were running, about this and that man with whom he had worked on the ranges or at the big annual roundups. But until the empty plates were pushed aside and chair legs scraped back and the men lighted their cigarettes, there were many little silences falling.

Mother Mary strove to kill silence as was her religion, and scolded at the slightest excuse, but for once she deceived nobody, and Babe Deveril forgot his wound, Marian Lee her trouble, in ready sympathy for

157

a mother whose pain at child-birth had been the smallest pain her son had caused her.

"If he does come," Babe Deveril told himself as they went back to the kitchen, "I'm goin' to take him back to the Two Bar-O with me and pull him up short. He's on the wrong trail and goin' fast, Charlie is."

Johnny Sanders' home was one of the good old elastic kind that has a place for every man and woman and horse that requires shelter. That night Marian Lee was shown into a little room where everything was cozy and comfortable, and where she was made to feel at home and to understand that she was to stay as long as she liked "me an' Johnny. An' don't you go an' let Johnny's outside fool you, neither. He looks crusty as a horn toad, an' he's just the best man an' the sweetest, most wonderful husband in the world!"

Babe Deveril and Stet Davis were given a bed together, and the low rumble of their voices continued indistinctly through the house until after the others had gone to sleep. For Babe and Stet were old friends and had much to ask and tell each other of the events of the many months since their trails had converged.

And Stet had news concerning Temlock and Verilees. At least he was sufficiently satisfied that these two were implicated in the recent wave of cattle rustling and horse thieving to wager such small items on it as his next month's salary, his saddle horse and hat. When a man is as confident as all that, there is a very strong likelihood of his knowing what he is talking about.

158

"It was the Roman Four outfit this trip," Stet said. "Close to a hundred big beef steers gone slick as a whistle an' every one of the bunch worth eighty dollars, or I'm a liar. It happened this way:

"Ches Mann got laid up along with a colt buckin' saddle an' all into a pile of rock, an' Crazy Bill Hancock got the job he's been hankerin' for for seventeen years as foreman. Ches was out'n his head an' flat on his back close onto ten day, an' in that time Crazy Bill cut an awful wide strip of loco weed. He said it was all foolishness, close herdin' like Ches was doin'; he called in a bunch of riders from the north end, said he reckoned the stock could roam free on the fringe of the Bad Country an' that was fence enough for anybody. He left one man up there to do the work of a dozen — Scotty McLeish — you know Scotty, Babe?"

"Sure. A good scout and worth a dozen men, too, when it comes to a fight. What happened?"

Stet grunted.

"A fight," he said shortly. "An' Scotty would have made good on it, too, I reckon. Only they didn't give him a white man's show. Six or eight of 'em, Scotty didn't know how many, dropped out'n the Bad Country on that herd, like a flock of buzzards on a dead steer. Only they come at night. Scotty woke up shootin' with both han's. But they got him an' it's nip an' tuck if he pulls through now. Doc Trip's workin' on him, givin' him horse liniment an' stuff."

"Did he get any of the rustlers?" demanded Babe.

159

"He don't know that even. It was too dark. He's sure he nailed one of 'em in the wing an' crippled him purty bad."

"Did Scotty know any of them?"

Stet hesitated and looked worried. Finally when he answered his voice was lowered so that Babe Deveril must lean closer to get the halting words.

"He ain't sure. That is, he wishes he wasn't sure, I guess, Babe. The fellow he shot in the shoulder wasn't much more'n a kid, nineteen maybe, sandy hair, loose jointed —"

"You don't mean —" began Deveril, his brows gathered, his tone as troubled as Stet's.

Stet swore swiftly. "Ain't it hell, Babe? Mother Mary'd most die if Charlie didn't come home tomorrow."

CHAPTER
FIFTEEN

Mary Sanders, up late the night before in seeing that her guests were made comfortable, in doing what ranch skill and a woman's instinct told her how to do for Babe Deveril's wound, in taking time for a last cheery word and a good night kiss for Marian, was up and about earlier than usual this morning.

She had dressed and slipped quietly out to the wide porch of the range-house before the misty darkness of the dawn had thinned in the east. She had stood there long alone, looking with an eagerness that was wistful and tender and anxious toward the road which skirted the Frying Pan and turned in at the lower gate.

"He'll come," she had whispered, her eyes suddenly as misty as the coming dawn. "Oh, I know he'll come! God is good after all. An' Charlie's never forgot. An' he's a good boy."

Then she hurried to the kitchen, that everything might be ready when he did come. It seemed that there was a particular way in which everything should be done this morning; the coffee must be made just so, the bacon cut into short rectangles, whereas it was usually fried in long strips, the biscuits to be Mother Mary's best.

She skimmed a big pan of milk and set away in a secret corner of the cupboard a little pitcher that held the cream of the cream. She had gone into the yard to collect eggs and had hidden the two biggest, freshest looking — they were all laid the previous day — at the side of the little cream pitcher when her husband came into the kitchen.

"Good mornin', Mary Girl," Johnny Sanders said rather softly for him. He came to her and put his arms around her and kissed her. "You're just the finest little woman this side of heaven, an' here's hopin' you have a hundred more birthdays, all better'n this!"

Whereupon, having made his annual oration, Johnny Sanders reddened with his annual embarrassment, Mary with her annual pleasure, and they drew apart like two guilty children as Babe Deveril and Stet Davis came into the room.

"Mother Mary!" chided Stet. "Here you are with another birthday an' a-flirtin' with ol' Johnny before breakfast, like you was just come sixteen! Johnny, quit bein' a hog an' takin' all Mother Mary's blushin' kisses."

And he in turn gathered her into his arms, picked her up, her feet clean off the floor, kissed her resoundingly and set her down at the other side of the room where he had carried her bodily.

"You scamp!" she cried, laughing at him and slapping his face with her open palm, so that both Stet's face and her hand reddened. "Don't you know no better'n to treat your Mother Mary like that?"

162

Babe Deveril too came forward; Babe too kissed her and wished her all the good, God-filled years to come that she so rightly deserved, which was a long eternity of them. And then she chased them all out of the kitchen, slamming the door at their backs, scolding and laughing, and when they were gone she went back behind her closet door again.

"He'll come today," she whispered. "I know he'll come."

And when a moment later Marian came into the kitchen to bring the fourth kiss of the morning and the fourth hearty well-wishings, Mother Mary was as gay and talkative as it was her custom to be.

At the breakfast table her cheeks were a little flushed, her eyes brighter than usual with the eagerness and anxiety still looking out of them, and at every little sound from the yard she started and looked out. And yet the breakfast was eaten, the dishes washed and put away, the morning coffee cold — and Charlie Sanders did not come.

Some of the boys came up from the bunkhouse before beginning their day's work to speak their blunt, short-worded greetings, having remembered the day this way for many years. They brought many little, useless things, which they had bought for her upon the last trip to town, bestowed them awkwardly and good-humoredly, and after a brief chat with Stet and Babe Deveril, and many swift and often lingering looks at Marian Lee, went back to the corrals. And Mother Mary thanked them all and blessed them all and scolded them all, and they went away laughing. But in the corrals their faces were grave.

"Somebody just nacherally oughta kill Charlie," one of them growled with much emphasis and accompanying profanity, "before he kills her."

That day Marian found her quick opportunity to repay this woman for much of her kindness of yesterday. For, while Babe Deveril and Stet Davis could only pretend not to see the trouble which grew in the misty eyes with each passing, empty hour, Marian had the woman's way of mutely acknowledging that she understood, of giving out her sympathy wordlessly, or bringing a certain slight comfort into a weary day.

"But he'll come, Miss Marian!" Mother Mary cried more than once. "Oh, I know he'll come!"

Johnny Sanders, a man who did not know the meaning of an idle day, was not to be seen about the place an hour after sunup. Babe Deveril and Stet Davis withdrew from the house and went down to the corrals, where they sat hour after hour, smoking, talking, planning.

Babe Deveril's one chief business in life just now must be to get well; his wound had not had a chance to heal, and he must give it that chance. He was optimistic about it, as it was his nature to be concerning all things, and he believed that a few days of rest here would put him in such shape that he could do his day's riding and could count on a steady hand when the need came.

164

And the need would surely come, and come soon now. For he thought that he could put his hand on Crag Verilees with little trouble, having stumbled into the watered valley in the Bad Country. And then, too, the men of the Roman IV were ready to lend a hand; Ches Mann, up and about again, was doing something beyond swearing at Crazy Bill Hancock, and was looking for his lost cattle.

"We can find them, every hoof and tail of them," Babe Deveril said positively, "right in that valley in the Bad Country! I've had time to figure it all out, Stet. Remember how the country stretches, rocky and dry, and too hard to dent to an elephant's track pretty near all the way into Larkspur? They get the stock into the Bad Country and they hide signs, and it's a job, but not such a powerful bad job either, not for the gang of twenty or thirty men Temlock and Verilees can get into line in two days' time.

"They herd 'em close in the valley long enough for the first excitement to flare up and burn down like a fire sinkin' for want of fresh fuel, and then they drive at night along the gullies leadin' down into the yards below Larkspur.

"Looks simple," grunted Stet. "A couple of crooks in Temlock's pay at the railroad, a sweaty night's work, an' the whole string slippin' along the rails, headed east an' to Chicago. An' they get time in the valley to blot the brands, too. It looks simple. Only we oughta stop their little play this trip. Huh?"

"Yes. How long a vacation are you takin' from the Wagon Wheel, Stet?"

Stet colored a little and his eyes dropped to his cigarette.

"Long's I want," he returned quietly. "I thought maybe I was ridin' a long trail when I set out, an' I sent word to the ol' man he better not look for me real soon."

"Then you're the man to do the work now. If you'll strike out for the Two Bar-O and carry the word, you can pick up a dozen punchers there who will be glad to get into the game. Ride from there to the Roman Four and you'll scare up some more; Ches Mann'll bring along every hand he's got."

"There's a half dozen boys from the Wagon Wheel who'll be sore on me the rest of their mortal lives if we don't let them in on the play," Stet added.

"We'll need all we can get," Deveril assured him. "I don't know how many men are in on the steal, but you can gamble that they are not doin' this sort of work with less than a couple of dozen. Men in their line of business are always expectin' something to break, and they'll be on the lookout for trouble. It's not goin' to be an easy matter, Stet, to wipe that gang out."

Stet got to his feet and, making no answer, stared out across the low-lying hills toward the Bad Country. And then his head turned a little and his eyes went to the house. As he turned, Marian came out on the porch. Stet Davis saw her.

"You'll just stay here until we get back?" he asked Babe Deveril colorlessly.

Babe Deveril's eyes, too, had gone to the house. For a moment then the two men looked into each other's

166

faces as they had looked the night before. Only this time they did not turn away from each other.

"It's my only play, Stet," Deveril said slowly. "I've got to be in at the showdown — you know that. Somebody's goin' to get Crag Verilees this time, an' it's got to be me! I — I don't like the job, Stet, of waitin' here, doin' nothin' —"

Stet Davis cut him short with an unpleasant laugh.

"Oh, you'll find plenty to do," he said shortly. "While I go chasin' off acrost the country doin' the dirty work, you'll —"

He broke off suddenly, his eyes darkening. Babe got slowly to his feet, his own eyes frowning.

"Look here, Stet," he said, his tone low and measured. "There's no sense in a man goin' and makin' a mistake just because —"

"Mistake?" Again Stet laughed shortly. "I guess I ain't makin' no mistake this time. There's times when a man'll play fair and square; there's times when the game is too big for him to play square with a frien' an' he forgets —"

"Stet!" There was a quick note of anger in Deveril's voice now, a note of warning. "Are you crazy, man?"

"Crazy?" Stet eyed him coolly. "Me? Maybe I am. I don't know whose business it is anyhow. I do purty much as I damn please an' I say purty much what I mean. Maybe you've noticed that? Anyway, if I am crazy, I ain't a fool, an' don't you go thinkin' I am. Now there's work to be did an' I'm goin' to do it. I'll carry the word an' I'll get back here inside twenty-four hours. 'Cause I'll send another man on the jump with the

167

word from the first place I hit an' I'll make it my business to ride back this way."

There the matter ended. Stet turned abruptly and went into the barn for his horse. He saddled quickly, swung up into the saddle and, with no word, no single look toward the man he had left in the corral, rode up to the house. Babe saw him rein in there, call a short good-by to Mary Sanders and the gray-eyed girl at her side. The frown in Deveril's eyes darkened when he heard Stet's voice, lifted and meant to carry to the corrals, saying:

"I'm comin' back real soon, Mother Mary. I got business up this way."

And he was gone, racing into the south and with no backward look at the man in the corral.

Babe Deveril went back to his soapbox and his smoking, a little of Stet's bitterness rankling in his heart. He wasn't shirking and he knew it, and Stet ought to know it. He was a wounded man, badly hurt, and Stet was the one to do this work.

He was glad that Marian Lee was on the ranch, but he told himself savagely that that fact had nothing to do with his staying here while his old friend did the work that had to be done. And in a sudden flash of anger he swore to himself that he would keep away from the house, that he would see very little of Marian, and that Stet when he came back would apologize or prove himself very little of a man. And then a shadow fell across him and he looked up quickly and found the girl at his side.

168

For a moment she looked at him wonderingly, her face flushing. For she had seen the anger in his eyes, and had seen in them no welcome.

"You don't seem the least little bit glad that I've come out to talk with you, Mr Deveril," she said a trifle stiffly. "I didn't intend to intrude upon your solitude."

"I'm always glad to see you," he answered her quietly.

She lifted her shoulders.

"If the eyes are the windows of the soul," she retorted, "your soul must look like a stovepipe inside. What's the matter?"

He flushed now, too.

"I've just been on the verge of quarrelin' with an old friend," he told her. "That makes a man's mouth taste bitter, you know."

"Quarreling with Stet!" in quick surprise. "Why what on earth do you want to quarrel with him for? He's just about the best, fairest, squarest fellow in the world!"

Deveril's eyes, beginning to soften now that she was with him, hardened at her words — almost Stet's own words in her mouth.

"I'm glad that you think so," was all that he answered.

She looked at him curiously.

"What's happened?" she asked gently. "I never saw you like this before. Why, I actually believe that you want to quarrel with me, too!"

"As a matter of fact I don't want to quarrel with anybody," he returned a bit stubbornly.

Womankind is, theoretically, very blind in seeing a certain thing which everyone else sees from the start. Perhaps Marian Lee was an exception to the rule, or perhaps something is the matter with the theory. At any rate a quick light came into her eyes, a light which, had Deveril seen it, might have hinted that she had her own guess at the cause of his bitterness toward Stet, and that she drew from it something of satisfaction, something of mischievous amusement, and that she did not treat it very seriously.

"You two remind me very much of two bad little boys," she told him, her tone seeking to be properly serious for scolding purposes and yet hinting at soft laughter. "Now, although you haven't been very nice to me, I am going to talk with you a while. For two very good reasons, Mr Deveril, sir! First, because I know Mrs Sanders wants to be alone, and second" — and now her voice was serious enough — "because I have something to say to you — something to ask of you."

He looked at her curiously. He even began to feel ashamed of himself, and pushed his box toward her and made her sit down.

"What is it?" he asked quickly. "Is it something I can do for you?"

"Yes." She sat down, made herself comfortable with her back to the corral and looked into his face, smiling a little. "You can if you will."

"And I will if I can," he told her earnestly.

"Are you sure? Oh, if you would only — But, listen: I know why Stet has hurried away and where he has gone. You are planning on getting a lot of cowboys together and on making war on the Temlock gang, aren't you?"

"How'd you know?" he demanded in surprise.

"Then I am right? I know that Stet brought word that the Roman Four has lost a lot of cattle, that a man was badly hurt and that it was thought that this was the work of Temlock and Verilees and their crowd. I know you, I know Stet Davis, and I guessed the rest."

"Well, you guessed right," he admitted. "And what —"

"Listen a minute: Those men are bad men, they are lawbreakers and it is right that they should be punished. But are you thinking more of the theft of the cattle or — or just of Crag Verilees?"

"Well?" he asked quietly.

"This is what you can do for me — if you will! You can see that those men are stopped in their lawlessness; you can have them handed over to the law! Let them be brought to trial; let them serve what terms the law imposes on them."

"Do you think," he asked her in surprise, "that they are going to give up when we call on them to? Do you think that Temlock is that kind? Or Verilees?"

"You can make them do it!" she cried impetuously. "You can get so many men with you that you can surround them, and they'll see that it would be madness to try to fight their way out! You can promise me that if you should see Crag Verilees —"

"What?" he said sternly.

"That you will not kill him! That you will give him a chance — one more chance! He is a bad man, oh, I

171

know that! I don't know what he has done to you, but I do know that it is an unspeakably horrible thing to kill a man! You think only of that thing you call the red law — that horrible, horrible lawless law! There is another law; you can have justice in the courts, and not have your hands all red with blood. I have done something for you, haven't I, Babe Deveril? Won't you do this thing for me — this one thing?"

"Marian," he said, his low voice grown very hard, "I would do anything in the world for you that I could do. You say you don't know what Crag Verilees has done. Go ask Mother Mary. She knows. And you are wrong about that other law — the law of the courts. There is only one law anywhere from one corner of the world to another to deal with a man like him, who has done the thing he has done. I am sorry, Marian, but —"

"But," she said coldly, "you are not sorry enough. You would kill him if you had the chance."

"Yes," he said sternly. "And I pray God I'll get the chance — soon!"

She had turned from him and was looking off toward the Bad Country. And then, before either spoke again, they heard a low cry from the house, a cry that came from a mother's heart and that choked in a mother's throat.

It was Charlie, Charlie come home for his mother's birthday. Just a boy, not twenty yet, a blue-eyed, brown-haired, slim, awkward boy. He slipped from his saddle, calling out a cheery "Happy birthday, mama!" With long swift strides he hurried to meet the little woman who sped down the steps and threw her arms

172

about his neck. He ran one arm, his right arm, about her, hugging her close, and his cheek was pressed to hers. His left arm hung useless in its sling.

"He, too, is shot!" cried Marian Lee hotly. "Here is some more work of your red law!"

"Here," Babe Deveril returned bluntly, "is some more work of men like Temlock and Crag Verilees! Two years ago Charlie was a decent boy. And now —"

She looked at him swiftly, her eyes commanding him to go on. But he only stared back at her moodily and remained silent.

CHAPTER
SIXTEEN

Babe Deveril knew who Marian Lee was. She was not
Marian Lee at all but Marian Ellston. He knew who
Ellston was and pretty much all about him, one of the
weakling brothers who, driven by a set of fates whom
doubtless some past deed of his had set yammering on
his fugitive trail, had wound up in a land of strong men.
He didn't belong in any such company. They slapped
him around; they put the fear of death in him; they
helped the yammering fates make him what he was
known to be now.

He was a clever man, might have been a brilliant
one. There were those in Hang Town and thereabouts
who could use a man like that — Temlock, for one.
Crag Verilees, perhaps, for another. Those three, the
black bear and the lean wolf and the jackal, hunted
together.

And Marian, Marian Ellston and not Marian Lee at
all, had fled into the poison-fanged wilderness of the
Bad Country, she alone save for an Indian whom she
deemed a faithful servitor and who was just a killer and
a snake. She had even repudiated her own name. That
meant that she was through with the community she
had set her back on, through with Ellston, with

everything that had to do with her past life. Starting out all afresh, that was what she was doing, she just a kid of a girl, all alone in the world. A world that could be gentle at times, as here at the Frying Pan ranch, but which so very, very often could be as cruel and heartless as the worst of the Bad Country.

What was she going to do? he wondered. Or rather, what did she think she was going to do?

A day drifted by, and another. Stet Davis was on his way, learning what he could learn, rounding up a crowd of rough-riding ranch men who at the drop of the hat would tie into the Temlock-Verilees gang with all the joy in life. And meantime Babe Deveril loafed at the Frying Pan. He ate and slept and rested, and gave his wounds a chance to heal while he felt the old-time strength flowing back into his veins.

He confided in his solicitous hostess.

"Mother Mary, if I go on like this, eatin' most six dozen eggs a day, first thing you know I'll be cacklin' like that old Plymouth Rock hen of yours, or maybe crowin' like your little old bantam rooster. And you just go on coaxin' me to drink all that milk out'n your big pans with cream an inch thick on top, and I'll be mooin' like a moo-cow. You're sure spoilin' me so's pretty soon I won't be man enough to get up out'n a rockin' chair."

"You dry up, Babe Deveril," she laughed at him, "an' shet your eyes an' open your mouth an' gulp down this here eggnog! An' no cacklin' an' mooin' about it!"

"Milk *and* eggs, same time!"

"An' whisky!" she reminded him.

"That makes it sort of different." He grinned at her, and obeyed orders.

They were in the kitchen. From where he stood he could see through the door to the dining room and on through the big, shadowy sitting room, and on to the porch. There in the hammock were Marian and Mother Mary's boy, Charlie; they seemed deep in earnest conversation. Mother Mary stepped up to him to make out what he was looking at; a contented and peaceful smile softened her lips.

"That girl's one in a million," she said, and you could tell that she meant it.

"Only one million?" countered Babe Deveril. "Shucks, Mother Mary; make it anyhow ten million!"

"Hmf! That a lot of girls, Babe Deveril." She looked at him narrowly and, as she turned away, said "Hmf!" the second time.

"They seem to have a lot to say to each other," he offered idly.

"I'm glad! Babe, do you know, I think Charlie tells her more things than he does me! I think he tells her a lot of things — Well, you know" She was just a trifle uncertain for a moment; she didn't mean to admit that there was anything in Charlie Sanders' life that couldn't well be an open book to the great big, wide world. But she was no fool, was Mother Mary! She carried on; she said: "I think he tells her about all sorts of men he's met up with here and there, as any ramblin', high-spirited young boy will; men like — like Temlock an' Crag Verilees."

"I guess she knows 'em both."

"I know she does. She's told me. An' I'd be glad if Charlie talks to her about men like them two polecats, and she gets a chance to talk back to him!"

It was just then that Marian jumped up out of the hammock, her sudden removal of herself almost upsetting Charlie whom she deserted with a volley of light laughter, and came tripping indoors, through sitting room and dining room, straight on into the kitchen.

"I'm going for a ride," she announced. "It'll be sundown soon, and I love this time of day. Oh, hello, Babe."

She was rather casual with that hello of hers; just as though all of a sudden she had become aware of his existence, somehow giving him the impression that she'd be forgetting it again in two shakes.

"If you begged real hard, I might ride along," he said.

She shook her head.

"No thanks. Charlie said the same thing. You boys stay here and help Mother Mary, then she won't need me," and she gave Mother Mary a quick hug and a quicker kiss and a smile set with dimples, and ran out the back door.

She rode straight into the setting sun. She rode bare-headed, her hair about her shoulders, the faint breeze very softly fingering her curls. She put her head far back, tilting a rounded chin on a rounded throat against the sky. She shook out her reins and let her horse race. A long sweep of grassy prairie was underfoot; miles away in the west were the hills behind which the red sun would soon slip to hide away until it visited other parts of the world and took stock of other millions of young girls hugging their own problems, joys and griefs, to their breasts; until it came back bringing up an apple green dawn, all the way from China. She had it figured out that that was why the daybreaks had such lovely pale greens and blues in them, Chinese colors!

And when she rode alone like this, at times up early to watch the last star wink out, or in the gathering dusk as now to watch the first star swim into the sky, there was always tumult seething within her as she started, but generally there was peace in its stead as she drifted slowly homeward. Yes, Charlie had told her more than even he fully realized. There were things which he had not told her which somehow she understood better than he did. Temlock and Crag Verilees!

Temlock and Crag Verilees, and men like them. Charlie Sanders was only a boy, a mere boy — she did not stop to think of his age in years, did not estimate that by that measure he and she were about of an age! She had a tendency to mother him somewhat as Mother Mary mothered all creation that came within her ken. She saw how Charlie, like all boys, had done his hero-worshipping. And he had made a hero, to begin with, of Crag Verilees! Crag Verilees of the tall, lean and graceful body, of the handsome, arrogant face, of the slightly swaggering carriage. Crag Verilees first, then Temlock!

178

And she knew what already they had done to Mother Mary's boy, who was really good and true, fine and generous at heart — just a hare-brained boy. And she could guess what they still might do to him —

Men like Temlock and Crag Verilees! Her small fists clenched, hard and tight. Oh why, why were not men like that wiped clean off the face of the clean earth!

It was almost a prayer!

She tightened her reins, bringing her galloping horse down to an abrupt standstill; with unseeing eyes she stared into the west where the sun had gone down, where there was a great glory of sundown colors.

"Wipe men like that off the face of the earth!" That was what she had said within her heart. That was what Babe Deveril, forthright and honest, meant to do! He had killed Indian Pete. Was the Indian any worse, was he as reprehensible as men who knew so much more, men like Temlock and Verilees, who went on their cruel and merciless way, trampling weak men like Ellston down into the much, having their unbridled way with girls like Marian Ellston, killing little blab-mouths like Windy Bendish, robbing and thieving as they swooped along their devious trails, putting their brands, the brand of Cain, on boys like Mother Mary's Charlie?

Poor Charlie! There was that arm of his with a bullet shot through the flesh of it just below the elbow. It was mending, as what wouldn't mend under Mother Mary's loving care? It would soon be well again. Then what? Then there would be a Charlie growing restive, fed up with ranch chores, chafed by his mother's apron strings, thinking of the swaggering, man's-man Verilees,

179

a Verilees to clap him on the back and flatter him with his entrance ticket to Crag Verilees' fraternity; and a Temlock with a sinister, impressive reputation. What would happen to poor Charlie? And, after that, to Mother Mary? And, in his own way, to Johnny Sanders?

"Only — only I wish Babe Deveril didn't have to do it! Oh, dear God, isn't there some other way?"

She came tearing back into the house, her hair flying.

"Oh, I've had the loveliest ride!" She caught Babe Deveril by the arms. "Dance with me! I'll sing the dance music! The world is the nicest place ever!"

They stared incredulously at her as well they might! They had never seen her in a mood like this — nor had anyone else, Marian Ellston, included! Thoughts, fears, hopes, weird fancies had all crackled through her brain like shreds of lightning so that her whole being was electrified, so that she was certain of nothing, afraid of much, shivering inwardly with a sort of thrill in the shiver, feeling herself to be a small chip hurtling along on a mighty, boisterous river, the river of life with its pools and whirlpools, with its rapids and slowly moving, quiet currents, with its hidden snags of rocks and its embowering, lovely trees.

She didn't quite know all the things she was saying. She said:

"I want to hold myself back from going out and doing what I want to do! I want to lock myself up so that I can't run and load up my old double-barreled shotgun and — and burn down some folks I've heard about! You dance with me, Babe Deveril! Swing me off my feet —"

She began to cry and ran out of the kitchen.

Mother Mary shook her head and wiped her eyes on the hem of her apron.

"That poor girl's ready to blow up," she said, her voice hushed. Babe Deveril, all at sea, was staring after the vanished girl; Mother Mary shook him by the shoulder as one would do to awaken a sleeper. "You be good to her, Babe! I can sort of feel what she's feelin'. You just be good to her, no matter what!"

That night, after supper a laughing, rosy-cheeked, sparkling-eyed Marian Ellston strolled down to the creek with Babe Deveril.

He showed her his two favorite stars.

"Those are *Los Ojitos de Santa Lucia*. The Little Eyes of Saint Lucy," he told her.

"I love them!" said Marian.

They had very few words to say that night. In a way, some of the things they might have said were spoken for them by the night itself, still and serene, lofty and at peace, with its lip at the great bowl of infinity. The breeze whispered and the creek murmured, and there were the stars. "*Los Ojitos de Santa Lucia!* I love them!"

But before he said good night, Babe Deveril did say this:

"Remember the place I told you about, what I call My Valley, where there's lots of green grass and free water runnin' wild? Remember how I said I'd like to

181

take you there sometime? Good night, Marian. I'm takin' me a little ride early in the mornin'."

For just a second he held her hand, then he walked away. She crushed her hand against her lips — she wanted to call after him — She knew where he was riding! But what could she do, what could she say?

She stood a long while where he had left her on the porch. Her eyes were lifted to the stars. They found again those stars of his —

CHAPTER
SEVENTEEN

It was night, moonless, starless, pitch black in the Bad Country. Babe Deveril, his horse waiting for him in a hollow upon the south side of the ridge, was making his stealthy way forward on foot, drawing closer at every silent step to the light he saw burning down there in the little hidden valley.

When he left the Frying Pan, Stet Davis had not come back; evidently as Davis rode his wrath had cooled, his vision had cleared and he himself had ridden upon the business of carrying word and gathering men. And while Deveril grew restless in the enforced idleness of waiting for his wound to heal, the punchers had not come.

Only later was he to learn that Ches Mann of the Roman IV had been drawn away upon a false scent, cleverly placed for him; had followed a fruitless trail and had sent every man he could get his hands on riding toward the south plains.

So at last, fearful that the herds which he was so certain had been driven into the hidden valley would be driven on and out before he could come to them, Babe Deveril rode back into the Bad Country as he had ridden before, alone. Some part of his strength had come back to him; his hand was steady again, and there was urgent work to be done.

"You are going after Crag Verilees?" Marian had said to him quietly down at the corral at the Sanders ranch.

"I am goin' to see if I am right and if Temlock and Verilees have hidden the cattle in the Bad Country," he had evaded her.

"And if you should find Verilees?"

He had had nothing to say. She had turned from him and he had gone without saying good-by. And then Marian Lee had gone quickly to Mary Sanders and had asked her what the thing was which Crag Verilees had done that had drawn him and Babe Deveril into such an implacable blood feud. Mother Mary, her face suddenly as hard as her husband's, told the story, a wretched story of wrong done a woman by a man who was merciless, and Marian Lee shuddered less at the account of the double murder which followed than at what went before.

The woman had been the young wife of a friend of Babe Deveril's; wife and husband had been coolly shot down by Crag Verilees. Oh, yes, he had been accused and arrested and tried. That was last year. And in the courts of law a lawyer — Marian was spared the knowledge of who that lawyer was — had connived with a crooked judge, and Crag Verilees had gone free. But now the evidence was in the hands of Babe Deveril and there would be no bribing this time.

Then Marian Lee had run out on the porch again, hoping that Deveril would turn, that she might wave her handkerchief to him.

184

But he had not turned.

And now, in the thick darkness which lay over the Bad Country, Babe Deveril was making his slow, guarded way toward the light that burned in the dugout. He knew already that he had come in time. Borne upon the faint breeze, there came to him from the north end of the valley the lowing now and then of a restless cow.

"There's a chance," he told himself, "that these fellows have worked this game so many times they're gettin' a bit careless. They'll have night-herders on the cattle but they're apt to leave this end open. And there's the chance that Temlock and Crag Verilees are both still here."

He made his way closer to the dugout, so close to the cliffs that the back of his right hand, feeling the way, never lost the touch of them. And presently he heard voices, a low, droning, indistinct monotone from the dugout.

The door and the little square window were both open; there was plenty of light from two candles stuck into the necks of bottles and set on a box serving as a table. From where Deveril stopped, not twenty steps from the rough building, drawn back a few paces from the wall of cliffs, he could look into the room.

And there were the two men whom most of all men he wanted to find. Temlock sat, his heavy shoulders stooping, upon a rude camp stool, his elbow touching the box upon which a candle burned flanked by a bottle half full of red liquor. Crag Verilees lay upon his back on the little bunk, his hands clasped behind his head, his lean, wolfish face lifted into the light, the sneering silent laugh characteristic of the man showing the cruel mouth twisted, the lips drawn back from the sharp teeth.

They were in the light, Babe Deveril in the dark. He could, in a flash of time cover them both with his two guns, calling on them to throw up their hands. He cursed himself for a fool; the one thing to do was to shoot without warning, to kill Verilees as he lay there unsuspecting, just as you'd kill a rattlesnake. That would have been Crag Verilees' way; that was the end which Crag Verilees deserved. And yet he could not do the thing that way; the best he could do was give Verilees an even break — and then kill him.

But first he must move a little to the side so that he came on them from the door; the window was not large enough. A swift movement on the part of the men within would carry them out of his line of vision. Then all they had to do was knock the candles over to make their position as secure as his own, leaving them with a two-to-one advantage.

He had both revolvers in his hands now. He began to move to the side, seeking a position squarely in front of the door, when the thing that Verilees was saying stopped him.

"You got the savvy all right when it comes to a cattle deal." Crag Verilees laughed. "But when it comes to a female girl you ain't got no more sense, Temlock, than a newborn bedbug."

Temlock glared angrily at him.

186

"It's my game an' I'm playin' it my way, Verilees," he said shortly.

"You ain't playin' it to win very fast," laughed Verilees, undisturbed by the other's tone. "You ain't got your dame, an' you don't know where she is, an' you're just takin' fool chances of gettin' us all in a tight hole where we'll have to shoot our way out an' run for it."

"What do you mean by that?" demanded Temlock sharply.

"Just what I say," Verilees answered him coolly. "You're gettin' that little shrimp of a law crook mixed up in our play just so you can put the screws on him an' get his girl. Hmf! Shows what you know about females, anyway. He could talk an' threaten all year an' she wouldn't pay no more attention to him than she did in Hang Town after the dance."

"I ain't askin' for none of your wisdom on that deal," growled Temlock. "I usually know what I'm doin' an' I do it my way."

"Oh, all right. Have it your way." Verilees sat up and reached out a long arm for the bottle. "Don't get touchy. All I was sayin' —"

"You was sayin' that I'm takin' chances by lettin' Ellston in. How's that come in, huh?"

Crag Verilees drank deeply and put the bottle back before answering.

"There's sixty-seven diff'rent kinds of crooks, Temlock. Among 'em there's crooks that has got sand an'll stick by a pal, an' there's crooks as is cowards an' would squeal in a minute to save themselves from gettin' a little finger hurt. That's Ellston's kind."

187

Temlock laughed.

"Look at that, Crag," he said with a trifle more of good humor in his heavy voice. He jerked a little, fat pocketbook from his hip and tossed it to the couch. "Guess you didn't know my system, huh?"

Verilees looked a moment at the book, glanced over its entries, unfolded a couple of papers, ran his eye over them, returned them to their place and tossed the pocketbook back to Temlock.

"That's nothin'," he said contemptuously. "I know what you got. You made him sign for some of the money, an' made him say how it come from sale of cattle we rustled. An' you think you can keep his lyin' mouth shet with a little piece of paper? That's the way you try to make sure of all the men, an' with most of the others maybe it's all right. They're square anyhow an' you don't need it. But Ellston?" He jeered. "Suppose he was took sick an' was goin' to die; suppose he'd squeal his little head off?"

"If he gets hurt," snapped Temlock, shoving the book back into his pocket and stuffing a big handkerchief down over it, "he'll die so damn quick he won't have time to squeal! I'm watchin' him, Verilees."

As the men grew silent again, Babe Deveril moved a cautious few steps farther toward the front of the dugout. Step by step he made his slow way, reckless of the chances he was taking if perhaps a third or fourth man of the gang might be sleeping in his blankets somewhere outside, within hearing distance.

And then, just as he came to a spot from which he could look in at the open door, just as he was ready to

188

call softly, "Up with your hands!" he stopped dead in his tracks, listened a moment and drew back again, swiftly, into the deeper darkness from which he had stepped. For he had heard the noisy clatter of hoofs racing up from the south, and frowning into the blackness he made out the running blurred forms of two horses.

"Stet Davis and Ches Mann!" was his first quick thought. But instantly he realized that Stet and Ches, had they been alone, would not have ridden in this headlong fashion into the valley, the noisy approach warning anyone who might hear.

It would be two of the Temlock crowd.

And then, in another moment, he made out that there were not two men but just one and that he was leading the second horse. Deveril drew still farther back under the cliffs, again commanding a view of the window. He saw that Temlock and Verilees were on their feet, their hands at their hips. He saw the racing horses come on, saw them stop at the dugout door, saw a man throw himself from the saddle and hurry forward. Babe Deveril, his curiosity keen, his anger high at the interruption, curbed himself to an enforced patience and waited and watched.

The new arrival hurried into the dugout. He was a lean, hard-faced fellow, quick-eyed and nervous in his manner, and looked saddle-worn and dusty as from a long, hard ride.

"Hello, Jim!" It was Temlock who spoke as he and Verilees went back to their seats. "You make enough racket for a dozen men. What luck?"

"Good," grunted Jim. "Gimme a drink." He took up the bottle himself, drank deeply, set it down, wiped his mouth on the back of his hand and ended, "I found her!"

"Where?" demanded Temlock eagerly.

"At Johnny Sanders' place. An' I found something else! Come here."

He turned abruptly and led the way back to the door, carrying a candle in his hand. Temlock and Verilees, evidently wondering, went with him.

He came to the two horses and held the light close to the side of one, the one he had led. It was saddled and bridled; a rifle was in its holster, and Babe Deveril knew the horse. It was the one he had ridden here tonight and left in the hollow upon the far side of the ridge.

"Well?" snapped Temlock. "What about it?"

"I picked it up on my way in," said the man swiftly. "Found it hid less'n a mile from here. What's it doin' here, huh? Where's the man as rode it, huh?"

Temlock and Crag Verilees exchanged quick, startled glances.

"Look at the brand," went on Jim hastily. He held the candle closer. "It's a Fryin' Pan horse! An' Babe Deveril an' Stet Davis was both at the Fryin' Pan less'n a week ago!"

Temlock's low, muttered curse was drowned by Verilees' sharp remark.

"Maybe it's Charlie Sanders —"

"But it ain't," cut in Jim positively. "Charlie is still at the ranch lettin' his mother an' Temlock's girl nurse his

190

sick arm. From all signs he ain't in no hurry to get well, neither," he ended with a short laugh.

In one flash of a second Babe Deveril saw and understood the hand Fate had dealt him, and he saw too the hand he would have to play out against the odds. So far he had played the losing game; he had lost a great deal when in a solitary land his horse hidden in a dark hollow had neighed at another horse and had been found by a Temlock man.

It would have been bad enough had he not had his wound, not yet healed, to contend with. Now, thinking clearly, coolly, and swiftly he saw that his chance of escape, should he seek it, had dwindled almost to the vanishing point. Temlock and Verilees knew that someone had ridden here from the Frying Pan, and they would be quick to look for Babe Deveril or Stet Davis; they would be on the lookout now. If they did not find him before morning, what chance would he have tomorrow on foot in a desolate country like this?

"They're only three — they're in the light and I'm in the dark — I've got to fight it out," he told himself grimly.

"If there's just one man" — Temlock was speaking, his voice lowered — "we'll get him before he can clear out. If there's more'n one, if they've tracked us after all, why — we'll clean the bunch out! Ride to the upper end, Jim, an' ride like hell! Tell the boys, an' tell Dick Barstow to get every man in the saddle an' down here on the run. The cattle'll look out for themselves tonight. Tell Barstow," Temlock added crisply, as Jim swung up into the saddle still warm from his riding,

191

"that I'm payin' any man of the crowd an extra hundred dollars if he nails the man this horse belongs to!"

The messenger drove home his spurs and raced away toward the north end of the valley, leaving the other horse, Deveril's horse, standing in front of the dugout. Verilees seized the dragging reins and jerked the animal toward him viciously.

"And now," was Deveril's instant thought, "it's only two to one!"

He had his chance with Temlock and Verilees, the chance to square an old score and to get his horse and ride, ride hard before Jim came back with Dick and the rest. But once again the words of the two men held him waiting, listening in order to learn all that he could.

"Anyway," cried Temlock triumphantly, "I've found her! She's at Johnny Sanders' place! She's mine to pick off when I'm ready!"

"Are you crazy?" snarled Crag Verilees. "Haven't you got enough trouble on your hands already without —"

"Shut up!" Temlock swung upon him angrily, threateningly. "I'm sick of your croakin', Verilees. When I want anything like I want that girl I go out an' get it. And I'm goin' to get her!"

"Yes?" sneered Verilees. "An' then goin' to be fool enough to marry her, huh? Oh, of course it'll be easy —"

"I'll make it easy! How? Damn you, Verilees, I'll tell you how! An' I'll give what orders I like, an' you'll obey 'em like the rest of the boys! Oh, I've had plenty of your back talk, more'n plenty! An' who the hell are you that I got to listen if I don't feel like it?"

"I'm the best man you got doin' your dirty work, an' you know it," returned Crag Verilees coolly. "I'm worth any six of your crowd, an' you know that, too. An' what's more I'm the only man in the whole damn outfit that ain't afraid of you! That's something! An' if you want to know it, Temlock, I'm gettin' just a little bit sick of my job!"

"Spit it out, an' hell take you!" cried Temlock. "If you got anything to say, say it!"

"Which I'm doin'," went on Crag Verilees in the same cool, insolent tone. "Here you hold a couple of dozen men in your hand, seein' you got more brains than they have, an' you get 'em signed up on a piece of dirty paper, sayin' they've took shares out'n a cattle stealin' or a hold-up.

"You go an' put over a stunt like this last one of rustlin' a hundred head off'n the Roman Four. You figure to slam them cows down in the yards at Larkspur, an' you get five thousan' bucks in gold for the deal. You shove half in your pockets an' let the rest of the boys scrap over the other measly twenty-five hundred. A dozen men in on this job an' they get about two hundred dollars apiece while you get two thousan' five hundred. An' me —"

"Yes, you!" snarled Temlock. "Ain't you satisfied?"

"No, I ain't! Who put this whole deal acrost? Who engineered it from soup to nuts, huh? An' what do I get? I get five hundred for riskin' my hide first and my neck next and all the time! Satisfied?" he snorted. "Don't be a damn fool, Temlock!"

"You're drawin' good wages," retorted Temlock. "You never made five hundred that quick in your life before I took you on."

"That's all right if I didn't. I can now. An' now, when it comes to a tight pinch, an' we're all in a mighty good way to swing to the first tree big enough for the job, you set up like a little tin god an' get the crazy hunch I'm goin' to let you send us all down the slide because you've got a hankerin' after a girl! I've told you already you was riskin' too much lettin' Ellston in. Now if you go chasin' after his girl —"

"You hit it right once," cut in Temlock, his voice sweeping arrogantly across Verilees' words, "when you said I got these boys where I want 'em because I got the brains. An' if you had the brains of the bedbug you was talkin' about, Crag Verilees, you might go after my job an' get it! But you ain't got a spoonful of brains to your name. You watch my play a few more years an' maybe you'll grow up!"

Verilees started to speak up, sharp and sudden, but Temlock cut him short.

"Now, listen to me, an' if you get tired listenin' say so an' I'll give you the chance you're aching for, to see if you're quicker than me on the draw! I say I'm goin' after that girl and I'm goin' to have her. Now, when I do anythin', maybe it's part hunch, but you can gamble it's most brains."

"I'm listenin'," sneered Verilees.

194

And Babe Deveril, waiting and watching, could see that these two men watched each other as closely as he watched them both.

"Which you generally do when I mean business," muttered Temlock. "Jim says she's at the Fryin' Pan. Jim says Deveril an' Davis both was at the Fryin' Pan an' is gone now. One's hereabouts — we got his horse. Where's the other?"

"What do you mean?" demanded Verilees quickly.

"I mean that I've thought that out already before you even noticed it! How'd one of 'em happen to come here? It's because he's onto our game! The game you engineered from soup to nuts! Why ain't the other with him? It's plain open an' shut. It's because he's rode down to some of the other ranges to get a crowd together!

"An' now what do we do? Ship our stock to Chicago? Rush 'em down to Larkspur on the dead run an' get 'em on the cars? Then these guys get the wires hot an' somewhere between here an' Chicago the shipment is stopped an' we get hell on both ends! That's what would happen if you had my job! You just wait till you grow to fit your breeches, Verilees."

"Chasin' after the girl will help, I reckon," muttered Verilees sarcastically.

"Who said it would? I said I'd get her, that's all. We can sit tight here an' let 'em close in on us, about a hundred strong an' with rifles. Or we can make a play that'll fool 'em. We can leave the cows here an' hit the trail down to the Fryin' Pan. The Deveril an' Davis' crowd'll meet there, it's fair bettin'.

"We can take our chance on gettin' to the Fryin' Pan first, an' being ready to hand 'em a surprise package out'n the doors an' windows when they ride up, or if they get there first we can play Injun with 'em on the trail this side, when they ain't lookin' for it. Then I'm ready to clear out and take a trip across the border. Anyway, we can wipe 'em out. An' if we set here or if we drive on to Larkspur they'll get the drop on us. Now, what you got to say?"

"I say you got sand in both your eyes," snapped Crag Verilees as coolly, as insolently as before. "If we get the cattle on the run now who's to know we shipped at Larkspur?"

Temlock stared at him curiously a moment.

"Can't you see through a glass window, Verilees?" he asked, and sounded disgusted. "Who's to know? Why, the man who put 'em wise to the whole play! The man *you* drawed in, thinkin' you'd have some sport makin' a kid go crooked. Charlie Sanders, that's who!"

Verilees jerked his head up quickly, the blood running for the first time into his cool cheeks.

"The dirty little snake!" he cried sharply. "If I don't twist his little neck! I'm with you, Temlock, for this time. An' while you take half your gang an' look for the jasper who's spyin' on us, let me take the other half an' ride to the Fryin' Pan! Don't worry, I'll take good care of your girl for you!"

CHAPTER
EIGHTEEN

Babe Deveril knew that the time, so long deferred, had come to act, to act swiftly, without hesitation and with never a false move. It was no longer just the matter of his own safety, for never had danger threatened Marian Lee as it threatened now. That one thought stood uppermost in his mind.

For Temlock and Verilees, warned now, pulling amicably together again in double harness because of a common peril, were of no mind to wait here for the arrival of the posse of cowboys for whom Stet Davis had ridden south. They would ride to meet them. They would come upon them unexpectedly at the Frying Pan or they would ambush them on the dark trail leading into the Bad Country.

It was too dark where Temlock and Verilees stood for accurate shooting. Jim had dropped the candle as he had obeyed Temlock's order to ride to the north end with his message to Barstow. There was just one thing to do: to wait a brief moment until the two men went back into the light of the dugout, or toward it, and then to call to them and to issue his commands.

They wouldn't quit cold, and he knew it. They would answer his voice with the guns ready at their hips. But he would be ready, too. And, because everything hung now on the squeeze of a trigger, it was up to Babe Deveril to make his first two shots do their business. Then he could swing up to his horse's back and run for it, dashing back to the Frying Pan with word of what he had overheard. It was the only chance for the men who were his friends, and for a girl who already was more than a friend.

And then came Verilees' snarling voice, and Deveril knew that he must not wait for better light, that it was up to him to take the chance that fate had already given him, and trust to that chance as well as to his own steady hand and eye.

"I'll hit the trail for the north an' follow after Jim," Verilees was saying. "If we got some ridin' to do, I'm goin' to change horses. I'll ride this here Fryin' Pan brute —"

"Put 'em up! High up, and damn quick!" cried Babe Deveril sharply.

He had both guns up, covering Temlock and Verilees as well as he could cover them in the uncertain light. As he spoke he leaped nearer and fired. For both Temlock and Crag Verilees, at the curt command, had plunged sideways into the deeper darkness, each answering his words with the bark of a revolver.

Deveril heard a grunt of pain at his first shot and knew that he had not missed Temlock. But Temlock's gun kept on spitting fire at him, and he knew too that he had not badly hurt his man. For a moment he thought that he had killed Verilees, for there came no second shot from him for several seconds.

Deveril fired at Temlock, or at the running, blurred blot in the blackness which he took to be Temlock. And then there came from the darkness into which Crag Verilees had disappeared a stream of bullets, five shots as fast as a man could pull the trigger — and Babe Deveril cursed under his breath as he fired back.

For Verilees had not shot at him, had not sought the small indistinct target when there was a larger, clearly defined one that he could not miss. He had fired at the big bulk of the frightened Frying Pan horse and the animal had reared, screaming, and had fallen heavily, kicking and pawing, unable ever to get up again.

"Take it slow, Temlock," sang out Crag Verilees' cool, laughing voice. "He's on foot now, an' we can pick him off most any time. It's Babe Deveril, that's who it is. An' we got him! The boys'll be here in two shakes."

For a moment the situation looked so utterly hopeless to Babe Deveril that he was caught briefly in the grip of indecision. And then anger, hatred and the thought of Marian Lee's desperate plight, and of the scarcely less risk run by Stet Davis and his following, riding into ambush, galvanized him, and he ran in closer, firing as he came. He heard Temlock and Verilees moving back before him, while their bullets hissed about him and plowed viciously in the dirt at his feet.

He sped toward their answering fire recklessly, for Verilees had said that the boys would come at any minute, and then what chance for Babe Deveril? The one thing, even if he were killed in the doing of it, was to drop Temlock and Verilees. With these men gone all

199

danger of attack on the Frying Pan would be minimized, in all likelihood would be averted entirely.

But in that darkness it was impossible for him to be sure of hitting a man ten steps away. And Temlock and Verilees kept a safer distance than that. They continued to play safe, to draw back as he came forward and they were separating so that in a moment, unless he watched his step, they would have him between them.

Then he heard the thud of hoofs thundering down from the north, and knew that Jim had heard the firing and was riding back, or that some of the night-herders, already mounted, had heard it and were racing to the dugout. In a moment there would be a dozen men against him and he would go down, riddled by bullets, leaving all his work undone.

He had counted his shots; he had fired ten times; he had one shot left in each revolver. And Temlock and Verilees would give him little time for reloading. He glanced quickly to the side and saw the candle burning in the dugout; almost at his side lay his horse, dead.

And then a quick thought that brought a gleam of hope with it came to him. Moving swiftly but silently now, suddenly ceasing his fire, he stooped over the Frying Pan animal, found his rifle still in its scabbard, found that he could draw it out, and then as the rifle came to his shoulder he fired.

The one candle left burning in the dugout was broken to bits; and a quick dash brought Deveril into the dugout as the pounding hoof-beats stopped not fifty yards away.

200

★ ★ ★

"I can hold 'em a while here," he muttered with grim satisfaction, as he moved to one side of the door, hearing the rattle of bullets against the wall. "And every little hour I keep 'em pluggin' away at me means Ches and Stet and the bunch will be an hour nearer the Fryin' Pan."

His knowledge of the interior of the little cabin stood him in good stead now. He could find the bunk easily in the darkness. He sat down, his rifle at his side, and hastily reloaded his revolvers. Now they were good for a dozen shots, and he would make the dozen shots count. His rifle cartridge belt was full, the magazine was full and he would spend lead carefully. For suddenly the basest of metals had become more precious than gold.

"He's in the dugout!" It was Crag Verilees' shout, and it rang through the night exultingly. "Who's that? You, Jim?"

"No," came a quick answer. "It's me, Andy Breen, an' Lefty. What's up? Who is it?"

"We'll know damn quick!" came Temlock's heavy voice. "It's Stet Davis or Babe Deveril, I think. Verilees says it's Deveril. Move aroun' to the other side, Lefty, so's he can't climb out'n the window if he gets the notion. Andy, you an' Verilees watch the door. I'm goin' to keep this side. Where's Jim?"

"He's rode on with the word you sent. The boys'll be down in no time."

Now Babe Deveril was ready for them. If only he could pick off Temlock and Verilees in that utter blackness!

201

"Come on, Verilees!" he shouted. "I've left the door open for you. You're right for once; it's Deveril, and I'm home to callers! Come on!"

"I'll come quick enough," answered Verilees coolly. "An' when I come in I'll scratch a match an' look down in your face — an' you won't see me!"

Deveril shot at the voice and heard Verilees laugh. On top of that unpleasant sound he heard another, even less welcome, the pounding of other hoofs from the north.

"If I could only keep 'em busy all night!" he muttered, "I wouldn't much care what happened in the mornin'!"

But how long could he keep them? That was the only question now. He thought of that while he ejected the empty cartridge from his rifle and threw a fresh one into the barrel. He was preparing his defense; he was trying to figure out exactly what form their attack would take. They would not rush him through the narrow doorway, for that would give him his one advantage and he could drop many a man of them before one of their chance bullets could find him in the darkness at the rear of the dugout.

They might try to burn him out. He had thought of that even as he rushed into the cabin. But he had thought, too, of the walls, part stone, and of the heavy logs, and of the roof made of thick slabs, dirt-covered. They would have their work cut out for them if they tried that, and he would give account of himself through the holes in the wall and through the window.

The door! He stepped to it softly, drew it shut and dropped into place the heavy wooden bar which secured it.

It was very quiet outside. He knew that Temlock was placing his men; he felt sure that their attack would begin in earnest in a moment. They knew that Stet Davis had ridden for men; they would be in a hurry to get this thing over with and to be in their saddles.

He broke down the bunk and dragged it to a far corner of the room, making a barricade of it. He made himself comfortable on the floor behind it, his rifle in his hands, his revolvers laid where he could find them quickly just beside him on the floor.

Now there was nothing to do but wait. He saw no chance of coming out of this thing alive, but none the less he must wait, must drag out the fight as long as he could, must make his lead and powder tell. He knew that there was a possibility of Stet Davis and Ches Mann coming before many hours; he knew on the other hand that he must not think of that, that they might not come for days.

He told himself that had only his own fate depended upon what he did he would not stay here like a rat in his hole; he would step outside and die in the open, die fighting, and that he would get Crag Verilees first. But now he must prolong the thing, he must stay here until they burned him out or until a chance bullet found him.

He was young, was Babe Deveril, and had little wish to die. But, now with the fighting spirit high within him, he had less wish to be thought afraid. They had him trapped; they knew that he knew this. And Crag Verilees might even now be laughing that evil, wolfish, silent laugh of his, picturing the trapped man going white and trembling.

And so Babe Deveril, reckless now as he had ever been, defiant and fearless, sent them his message to tell Crag Verilees and the rest that he was unafraid. There in the darkness, all alone, with death threatening him on every side, he put back his head and, keeping time with a thumb beating against the stock of his rifle, lifted his clear young voice in lusty, untroubled song.

He sang a song of the range, a song that was known from one end of the cattle country to the other, and his voice reached the high notes, sank to the low, soared upward again serene, steady, clear and richly musical. It was a song known east, west, north and south of the Bad Country, "The Cowboy's Finish":

"*Oh!* — I carve my meat with a bowie knife,
    An' I pick my teeth with the same;
An' I sleep with a rattlesnake wrapped roun' my neck,
    An' I set in most any old game.
Oh — I'm bad as they make 'em, I'm tough as they come!
    I'm a ramblin' ol' puncher who's done his las' spree;
I've rode my las' trail like a son-of-a-gun,
    Now On High I'll ride hard an' ride far an' ride free!"

***

He stopped, drawing his lungs full of the sweet air. It was a wonderful thing just to be alive, how wonderful he had never fully appreciated before! Well, he would make the most of what was left to him of life. He would live it out merrily; he would ride his last trail as a man should.

Outside the silence remained unbroken, undisturbed; it seemed to take on a new, sinister quality, to thicken and grow heavier, like a black velvet shroud. Then, as his song hushed, he heard a man laugh; he heard a heavy, raucous voice calling out something, though he could not catch the words, and Babe Deveril lifted his own voice lustily into the chorus. And at the first word of the refrain he heard other voices, voices outside, lifted in unison with his, and as he sang his blood tingled to hear those other men singing with him. They all sang shoutingly together:

"Whoop! Whoopee!
Rumble up, an' tumble up, an' crowd along the bars;
    Punch a little, loaf a little, hit your pace an' roam!
An' me, I'll be ropin' the Big Bear up in the stars;
    My Ol' Man in the Up Yonder has ordered me,
    'Come Home!' "

Again there came silence, that same heavy, ominous silence. It threatened in its very lack of warning. They had laughed at him, they had, in a spirit not entirely foreign to his, sung with him, and he knew that they had drawn nearer. He could tell that from their voices.

205

And now it was their business to kill him, to send him along that last trail; it was his business to kill them if he could, so that that long, last ride might not be lonely.

Then, suddenly, the silence was broken by a snapping volley of pistol shots and the rattle of bullets against door and walls.

Babe Deveril saved his ammunition and while he saved it picked up the song again:

"*Oh!* I'm ready to ride, hell-bent, on the trail,
    On the Home Range where a fence-post is made with a star;
The last trail, the steep trail, the cowpuncher's trail
    When he's downed his last drink with his pals at the bar.
Oh! — the sun'll come up an' the sun'll go down,
    An' the boys'll hit town after work on a spree,
But me, I'm gone on where the ranges are wide,
    Where a man can ride hard an' ride far an' ride free!"

And, as another volley of shots came and the bullets tore their way through the door and window and the many chinks in the walls, throwing splinters in his face, he took up the chorus again.

And as before the voices of Temlock's men joined in lustily with him:

"Whoop! Whoopee!
Rumble up, an' tumble up, an' crowd along the bars;
    Punch a little, loaf a little, hit your pace an' roam!

206

An' me, I'll be ropin' the Big Bear up in the stars;
My Ol' Man in the Up Yonder has ordered me,
'*Come Home!*'"

"Hello, Babe! Feelin' fine?" came a deep voice from outside. "You ol' son-of-a-gun, what did you want to go an' get mixed up in this party for?"

"That you, Emmet Wood?" returned Deveril carelessly. He thought he recognized the voice. "I sort of thought you'd gone crooked. Better keep back a little or I might hurt you by mistake," and he fired through the window in the direction of the voice.

Wood answered, first with a revolver, then by saying in an off-handed sort of fashion:

"Stop any of that lead? Say, Babe, your Ol' Man up yonder won't know you when you unsaddle at the Home Range, you'll be all mussed up so!"

"I was just wonderin'," retorted Deveril, shifting his rifle to his left hand and returning a revolver shot for Wood, "if you boys were goin' to let me die of slow starvation in here!"

Wood laughed and remarked to the man at his side:

"He's a game little devil, ain't he, huh?" And then it grew silent again. Deveril kept on the alert, his eyes flitting ceaselessly from door to window, his ears straining for any little sound to tell him where a man was coming cautiously nearer, to give him a hope of firing a shot that would find its mark.

"Temlock'll be gettin' tired of this," thought Deveril. "And it isn't Craig Verilees' way of doin' business to wait all week. Something's goin' to break in a minute."

207

He reached a searching hand for the little cupboard in the corner near him, found a biscuit, made cowpuncher-style that morning, a bit of cold meat, and gnawed at them hungrily while he waited.

"A man might as well die comfortable," he thought. "And you don't die every night — maybe not even tonight!"

He whipped up his revolver and fired through the square of the window at a shifting shadow. A little muffled cry told him that he had not missed this time.

"That you, Wood?" he asked joyously, swallowing a bit of meat so that he could speak.

"No," came Wood's voice from a point farther to the right. "That's Andy. Hurt much, Andy?"

Andy's cursing voice told him to go to hell, and Andy's revolver spat flame and lead back through the window.

"I'm out of luck tonight!" laughed Babe Deveril. "But I never did have much luck shootin' coyotes in the dark!"

Then he heard the sound he had been listening for so long, the little noise that told him a man had crept close, very close to him from the side. He sat still, listening, trying to be certain that he had correctly located the noise.

It sounded as if a man were on the roof. But how could that be? He would have heard him before, when he climbed up the side of the dugout. The noise came again, and he knew. It was against the wall, just behind him, and close up to the roof. There was a long crack there, he had seen it many a time when he and Marian

Lee had been here together. The man knew of it and was creeping up to it to thrust a gun barrel through, to get him when next he fired and the flame from his gun showed his position.

Slowly Babe Deveril got to his feet. He knew that the slight sound he had heard was the scraping of a gun barrel against the wood as it was pushed through the crack. He drew a step closer, his eyes seeking for the tiny opening. But it was too dark, too black outside, for him to see anything.

"I'll have to guess again," he told himself sternly. "And it'll be bad business for me if I guess wrong."

Then, when he thought that he had found the place, he pushed both revolvers out in front of him, finding a chink between the logs just below the spot where he thought the crack to be, and as he moved them he fired both together. There was an explosion just above his head, a scream from the outside wall and the sound of a heavy body falling heavily.

"If it was only Temlock!" he muttered aloud.

But it was not. For a moment later he heard Temlock's heavy voice calling a curt command to his men to fall back a little for consultation. There would be a quick shifting of the campaign and Deveril tried to figure out, as he crouched there in the quiet darkness, what it could be.

He had wounded Temlock with his first shot of the evening, but not badly. He had scratched Andy, but Andy had been able to shoot back. He had hit that other man who had stolen up to the dugout wall and had, perhaps, put him out of the fight. Still there were a dozen or more men out there to be reckoned with. Now they were drawing together to take orders from Temlock; Temlock had worked out his plan, and smashing action would come swiftly.

"And I'm to wait here like Mr Rat in his hole until they get ready to blow me to thunder!" grunted Deveril disgustedly. "Not if I know it!"

He moved swiftly and noiselessly to the front of the small room, quietly lowered the bar from the door, opened the door inch by inch until it had swung back a foot or more, keeping his body protected by the heavy panel lest Temlock had left a man to watch for this thing. But, constituting a dark blot against the dark night, he made out the forms of Temlock's men gathered close together some fifty paces away.

"If they're goin' to do any secret plottin'," muttered Deveril as he opened the door another cautious six inches, "they're going a lot farther away to do it!"

He went down on one knee, knowing that in the darkness they would have a tendency to shoot high, and as fast as he could work lever and pull trigger he poured six shots into the compact shadow.

A bellowing yell of rage — it was Temlock's unmistakable voice — was followed by a scream of pain and a volley of curses, an accompanying volley of rifle and pistol shots, and a stinging pain in his arm — he cursed joyously when he told himself that it was only his left arm, anyhow, and only a flesh wound. He shoved his rifle back behind him into the dugout and began emptying his revolver at the dim, blurred, scattering shapes.

210

"That'll make you hunt your holes, you pack of coyotes!" he called gaily to them, the pain in his arm forgotten in the joy of pelting lead after the scampering, shadow black shapes.

And being part daredevil and all cowboy in all that the good old word connotes, his fighting blood hot in him, his youth rampant, his recklessness unleashed, as he fired he broke again into his rollicking song, the pauses in his ballad punctuated by pistol shots:

"*Oh!* — I'm shot full of holes, I'm drippin' with gore,
   I'm a ramblin' ol' puncher who's done his las' spree!
I've rode my las' trail like a son-of-a-gun,
   On High I'll ride hard an' ride far an' ride free!"

CHAPTER
NINETEEN

At last the solid ebony blackness of the night was broken a little. A high wind had torn here and there a rift in the cloudbank above.

A pale moon and dim stars threw a faint, ghostly light in the hidden valley.

The firing had ceased. Temlock's men, those of them whom Babe Deveril's lead had not struck deep, watched the dugout as the darkness thinned. There had come no answering fire to their last volley. The stillness which had shut down was like the stillness of death over the tiny cabin. But Temlock's men were suspicious, and they held back, ready at a sign to begin again their swift firing.

"He might be playin' possum," snarled Crag Verilees. "An, then again he oughta be dead."

"The door's shet," returned Temlock, frowning into the murk of the night. "He's gone back inside, anyway. Most likely he's playin' possum."

He lifted his rifle as he spoke and poured a stream of lead into the door. There came no answer from within. And then . . .

Suddenly the silence that had followed Temlock's shots and short words was broken by a chorus of yells, the wild yells of cowboys riding into a fight, the hammering thud of flying hoofs drawing up from the south, and above the sudden uproar a lusty voice shouting:

"Hold the fort, Babe! Here we come!"

That was Stet Davis' voice ringing out like a clarion through the night. Stet Davis himself came riding at the head of twenty cowboys, racing down upon Temlock and Crag Verilees and the rest like a veritable cyclone of wrath and destruction. And then the dugout door snapped open and Babe Deveril leaped outside, his voice lifted joyously to Stet's:

"Come on, you old son-of-a-gun! You're sure welcome! Come on, you Stet Davis, and bring your friends!"

The steady pressure of the night wind bore back the clouds, the darkness kept on thinning, and Babe Deveril, standing straight and shooting fast, could see men everywhere running toward their group of horses.

But already the horses, frightened long ago at the din of battle, were plunging and dragging at the bridle reins by which a couple of Temlock's men were striving to hold them. They fought hard now as the new sounds tore through the night; they pulled back, pitching, rearing and kicking as their masters ran to them, as from the south the crowd of cowboys bore down toward them, shouting and shooting. And the men holding them had more thought of their own personal safety than for the safety of their companions. A very little margin lay between each one of them and a quick death, and they knew it.

Babe Deveril, firing at each running figure that his eyes could pick out through the darkness, saw that many of the horses had broken loose and were running free, with flapping stirrups and reins whipping about their forelegs. He saw a man catch a swinging bridle rein, jerk the horse about and swing up into the saddle. He saw the mass of his friends bearing down on them, saw that mass thin and widen as they spread out to cut off the wild flight of the rustlers.

And then he saw Temlock and Verilees, not twenty steps from him. He knew them from Temlock's great, thick body and Crag Verilees' long, lean frame, and from their voices. And he raised his revolver, took steady aim at the taller form, and heard the dull snap of the hammer as it fell on an empty cartridge.

But before he could drop the gun and jerk with his one good hand at the other in his belt, he saw something which held his arm. Temlock had caught at a horse running by him and his gripping hand had found the reins, had brought the animal to a snorting, terrified halt. There was not another riderless horse that Deveril could see. And Crag Verilees was at Temlock's side.

There was a chance for one of them — a chance for escape in the darkness, for a wild ride that might bring safety if the flying lead missed him. Temlock saw a lost game and saw his one chance; Crag Verilees saw the one chance as Temlock saw it, and already his hand had gone with Temlock's to the whipping reins.

"Let go, you fool!" shouted Temlock, his voice harsh with rage.

214

But Crag Verilees did not let go. Nor did Temlock call to him again. It was each man for himself now and scant enough hope for either of them. Temlock's revolver was in his left hand. He raised it swiftly.

Deveril saw the glint of the starlight on the polished barrel. Crag Verilees saw, and his own revolver, ready in the iron grip of his right hand, did not come above his hip as he fired.

The two men were still clinging to the reins; there was not the space of three feet between their big, panting bodies. And there was no measurable fraction of time between the two pistol shots.

The horse jerked, broke away from a weakening grasp and ran free, snorting its terror. Temlock and Crag Verilees did not fire a second shot. They were lying close together, very still, when Stet Davis threw himself down at Babe Deveril's side.

"Good God!" cried Deveril. "Did you see that, Stet? Temlock and Verilees — they have killed each other!"

"The first time in their lives either one of 'em ever did a decent thing!" said Stet Davis sternly. "They've both did something I never thought either of 'em ever could — they've earned a decent funeral!"

Then he turned from them as if he had forgotten them, as perhaps he had; turned to Babe Deveril and slowly put out his hand.

"I was a fool the other day, kid," he said quietly. "You know what I mean. It was because I was sore, Babe, an' —"

"Forget it, Stet!" cried Babe, and gripped the proffered hand. "We were both damn fools, an' —"

"An'," went on Stet hurriedly, to have the thing over with, "it was because I was jealous. I heard her talkin' to Mother Mary about you, an' — Oh, hell, Babe! What's the use wastin' good time? If I was you I'd take a horse an' burn the earth getting' back to the Fryin' Pan. Somebody's awaiting for you, old-timer."

Babe Deveril, suddenly bereft of the words which he wanted, stammered something unintelligible.

"Oh, shut up!" said Stet, giving his hand a final hearty squeeze. "Get ready to do some ridin'. There's two mighty fine ladies back to the Fryin' Pan, but one of 'em's lonesome! Mother Mary's so busy bein' happy that Charlie's back — an' I guess he's come to stay, havin' took a brace an' swore he'd travel straight if us boys would give him the show an' — Oh, shucks, Babe, why don't you hit the trail?"

And Babe Deveril, having taken time to shift a certain pocketbook from Temlock's pocket to his own, found a horse and hit the trail.

"I'll tear up the evidence against Ellston," he thought, "Marian need never know."

"An' me," muttered Stet Davis, looking a little wistfully after his departing friend, "why, I'll jus' nacherally buy that hundred-dollar fiddle for a weddin' present!"

Whereupon he sighed and made a cigarette and then went out to meet Ches Mann.

"Where's Babe?" asked Ches quickly. "Ain't hurt much, is he?"

"Nope," returned Stet cheerfully. "Not much, I guess. Only recent he was shot right square through the heart, that's all!"

And Ches Mann laughed understandingly.

"By a girl, you mean?" he chuckled.

"By a girl," said Stet Davis. "Yep. A real girl."

CHAPTER
TWENTY

Babe Deveril," said Mother Mary, "you tell *me* something!"

They were sitting in the warm kitchen at the Frying Pan ranch, a place redolent of the most pleasant aromas in the world — hot breads and cookies and pies and the like. Babe Deveril swore that a starving man would pick up strength and grow fat again just sitting there and smelling the good things, both past and present.

She had done the dishes and he had watched her with interest; of course he had made a bluff at helping her and of course she had threatened him with a hot dish rag. Now they sat and talked. Alone they were, for Johnny Sanders had taken up his lantern and gone out to the barn to see that the stock was properly fed and bedded down; and Johnny by now would probably be sitting on the top bar of the corral, giving them their chance to talk. A wise old boy, one who knew the two of them, was the taciturn Johnny Sanders.

"So you want me to tell you, huh?" said Babe Deveril. "I wonder what?"

She rolled her plump, brown arms up in her apron, sat forward on the edge of her kitchen chair and regarded him narrowly.

"Babe Deveril, you always goin' to be just a common, no-good, foot-loose cowpuncher? That all you got in that empty head of your'n?"

He looked back at her soberly; for once he answered her soberly and seriously.

"I don't know why you ask or why you care, Mother Mary," he said, "but the answer to that nosy question of yours is 'No.' Now, I'll tell you something, that bein' what you asked for at the jump-off."

And he told her, and she listened in a way that shut out all sounds of the rest of the world; she didn't even hear the noisy old clock ticking, didn't hear it making its preliminary, rusty-sounding noises like a man clearing his throat when it got ready to strike. He told her about the ranch — what he had called My Valley once when he had mentioned it to Marian Lee — and how he had had his eye set on it for a good seven years.

"I've saved up some money since then; not enough," he admitted, "but plenty to get started on."

He went sketchily into details. The place belonged to an old-timer, old man Bill Martin. Somebody, the Temlock crowd maybe, had raided him. They had driven off his stock, and had burned down his house and barn and outbuildings, raising merry hell with him and having themselves some drunken fun. Old man Martin had dug out; he had enough money left to live on; he was holed-up in a hotel down in White Rock; he'd be darned glad to sell out.

"The place will be easy to buy," said Babe Deveril. "It's the same as mine now. For a while, until a man got started, he could live on game and fish up there, with a few store groceries. Then he'd get somebody to go in with him to stock the place, goin' in on shares. Shucks! Like rollin' off a log!"

"Whyn't you talk to Johnny?" said Mother Mary.

He grinned broadly at her.

"I'm talkin' to you, Mother Mary!" He chuckled.

"You're a rascal, Babe Deveril!"

"But, look here; you haven't told me anything. About Miss Marian. You said she'd gone; that's all you said!"

Mother Mary tightened the apron wrapped about her stout arms.

"That's all I got to say," she retorted, and tucked in the corners of her mouth — tight!

"Where did she go? Come on now, tell me!"

"Nope. Won't. Promised not to tell. Not to tell anybody. Especially you. Charlie, he went along with her."

"*When* did they go?"

"You don't get me into any traps, Babe Deveril! Now you go on, finish tellin' me things. All about what happened up there in that thieves' valley in the Bad Country."

He told her, making it as brief as he could, sketching only the results of the episode, then saying:

"Temlock and Crag Verilees are done for. They'll never ride again."

"Babe Deveril, you killed 'em! You shot both of 'em down!" She looked proud of him — and afraid. She rolled her arms up tighter than ever.

"No such thing." He told her how the two men, desperate, each seeing his one chance alone, with a

220

horse between his knees, had fought over the one horse to be had. He told her how they had shot each other down. He said, "The best job they ever did, either one of 'em! We ought to put up a fine tombstone over their grave; write on it, 'Us fellers, Temlock and Crag Verilees, we killed each other, each of us tryin' to steal the same horse! Anyhow, we did a good deed.'"

"You're tellin' me the truth, Babe?"

"So help me," he said earnestly.

She sighed; it was a long, deep sigh. "The Lord have mercy on their souls, Babe Deveril — an' the Lord have mercy on me for bein' downright glad! — What do you want of Marian anyhow?"

"You're awful nosy, huh, Mother Mary?"

"Want a cookie, Babe?"

She got up and brought a big pan of brown beauties, covered over with a snow-white dishtowel. He reached out with one hand and gathered them in; he stretched out the other hand —

She whipped them away.

"You're just exac'ly like you used to be when you was a dozen years old." She put the pan away and brought a pitcher of milk and a thick, earthenware mug. "Milk, Babe?"

She brimmed the mug and he lifted it to her as a man may lift a glass to a "Here's how." She sat down again and was about to say something when Babe Deveril, munching crisp cookies and washing them down with sweet milk, said, "She didn't go back to Hang Town again, did she?"

"I'll say not! Wild horses couldn't pull her back there!"

"She didn't run off into the wilds again, did she? Not into some crazy place like the Bad Country."

"Of course not. You know she wouldn't do a fool thing like that twice!"

"Maybe she moved along to some other ranch, huh?"

"Not by a jugful! And you know as well as I do that — Look here, you Babe Deveril! I promised her I wouldn't tell where she went, and a promise is a promise."

"What did you promise anyhow? Not to tell where she went, that was all, wasn't it?"

"Well, that's aplenty; that's all you want to know, young man!"

"You didn't promise to tell where she *didn't* go, did you?"

"What are you drivin' at? Gone plumb foolish, boy?"

"Did she go in to Rocklin for instance?"

Mother Mary's eyes lighted up. She hid her smile, or almost hid it, with the corner of her ample apron!

"Nope," she said with a free conscience. That wasn't telling where she *did* go, that wasn't breaking any promise.

"How about Deep Wells? Didn't happen she went that way, did she?"

"Nope," said Mother Mary.

"Hm. Let's see." He ate another couple of cookies, had another long draught of his cool, fresh milk. "How about Red Rock? She might have headed that way?"

"Nope. I'm not sayin' where she went, 'cause I said I wouldn't. But it wasn't Red Rock."

"I wonder what's she's figurin' on doin'," said Deveril. "I wonder how she's goin' to get along. She didn't have a thousand dollars hid in her boot, did she?"

"She's right good playin' the fiddle," said Mother Mary, and looked him straight in the eye, as though she meant her eye to tell him things denied to her tongue. "She knows a whole lot about music; shucks, she can read dots on a page of music and play it right off. Music, I said. Yep, she sure knows a lot about music."

Babe Deveril left off worrying cookies for a time, while he chewed at his knuckles.

"Music, huh? Not playin' for dances; there wouldn't be dances often enough. Not — Say! Teachin' music!"

"You think you're smart, don't you," sniffed Mother Mary, but her eyes brightened.

Babe Deveril's grin became expansive.

"Say," he asked, "can she play a mouth organ or an accordion?"

"What do you want to know for?"

"I bet she can; I bet she can teach on 'em anyhow! And if she can — Man! In less time than it will take you to say John Robinson she'll have her anyhow about fifty cowboy scholars!"

"Maybe you figger on takin' lessons," sniffed Mother Mary.

"She didn't head down to White Rock, did she?" asked Babe Deveril.

Mother Mary looked at him steadily. Presently she answered.

"I promised not to tell where she went, Babe, an' I won't. Only if it chances you should ever meet up with that little girl or with my boy Charlie — You look out for 'em, won't you, Babe?"

Next morning early Babe Deveril headed down toward White Rock.

White Rock was no such populous city as to give you any great trouble finding your man — or your girl, as the case might be. Perhaps a thousand or twelve hundred souls, providing that all those who walked up and down had souls, resided there.

At any rate Babe Deveril had no trouble in finding what he sought.

First, he spotted Charlie Sanders. Babe Deveril had loafed about town, keeping eyes and ears open; he hadn't asked any questions. That wasn't his way, asking all sorts of questions; somehow they tipped a man's hand. His business was his business and he liked to keep it that way. He could be as patient as the ancient cottonwoods making White Rock shady, as patient as the still rocks on the hillsides, when it struck him that that was the way to play his game. And in the end, he saw Charlie Sanders holding up the corner of a ramshackle building, the Welcome House, with lean, languid shoulders.

"Hello, Charlie," said Deveril. "Let's go inside and have a beer."

Charlie Sanders came out of his apathetic droopiness with a start.

"Why, Babe Deveril! What in blue blazes you doin' down here to White Rock?"

They shook hands. They even rolled a couple of cigarettes. Then they went into the Welcome House and carried their bottles of beer over to a little card table.

They talked at random about this, that and the other. Babe Deveril had never a consequential thought in his head, you would have said. He was just in town on his way somewhere else.

But after a while Charlie, shifting his feet under the table, began the questioning — and before he was through, Babe Deveril knew all about Miss Marian Lee!

Charlie knew well enough that there had been something going on up in the little lost valley on the farther rim of the Bad Lands; he wanted to know the whole story and all the details.

Babe Deveril answered him idly:

"There was a kind of fracas up there, Charlie. You know about these two jaspers, Temlock and Crag Verilees? Well, they've been runnin' stolen stock up into that neck of the woods, holdin' 'em there a few days, sendin' 'em on to the railroad yards or some other place, dependin' on how things broke. Well, this time things broke bad for the rustlers, as both you and me know they always got to do, give 'em time. The gang is busted up, nice and proper. Temlock, he's dead. Crag Verilees, he's dead. Some of their other boys happen to be dead along with 'em. Any that got away won't show up in this part of the world, never, never no-more."

Charlie took a deep breath; he wiped the beaded sweat off his forehead.

"How's the arm, Charlie?" Deveril asked, as if voicing an afterthought. "Seems all mended."

"Babe," said Charlie as he wiped his brow with his fingers and gave his wet fingers a flip, "I'm goin' to tell you something —"

"No, you're not tellin' me anything, Charlie. You just do yourself your own bit of thinkin' — Say! Before long I'm sort of hopin' to have me my own ranch! How'd you like to trot along and work for me? Maybe you wouldn't get rich over night" — he grinned widely and clapped Charlie on the shoulder — "but I bet a man you wouldn't be gettin' your arm hurt!"

"Dammit, Babe, I'm for it!"

And they talked on. And one thing led to another as it generally does. And in due course Charlie mentioned Marian Lee; he just couldn't help it. Maybe Babe Deveril steered the conversation around into a trend from which it was quite the natural thing for Charlie's mind to slide down a certain groove. Anyhow, without Babe Deveril making a single remark that might be catalogued as a request for any specific information, Charlie Sanders told the tale.

Miss Marian was in White Rock. She was the most wonderful woman in the world. ("Woman, since when?" muttered Babe Deveril inwardly. "Just a little girl like no other girl ever was!") She had a little place, all her own. It had been a cigar store and lunch counter; it had belonged to Jake Ruff. Jake had got into a poker game and got shot up and had died from lead

226

poisoning. He owed money to the bank; the bank grabbed the corner cubicle. Now they rented it to Miss Marian for next to nothing a month. In back, behind a partition that she had wheedled the banker, old man Collins, into putting up for her, she had her bunk. Then there was another partition cutting the front of the place into two dinky rooms. In one Marian gave music lessons, certain hours. In the front — they had ripped the lunch counter and such truck out — she was running a millinery shop! Oh, that woman was a wonder, take it from Charlie.

And Charlie went in every day and swept the place out and helped her with whatever a strong-arm man could do.

"You don't have to tell her you saw me," said Babe Deveril when they got up to go.

"That's right. And — Say! You don't have to tell her I told you where she was!" said Charlie, bethinking himself belatedly.

Later, that same evening, Babe Deveril ran into Stet Davis, just blowing into town. And with Stet were a dozen other cowboys, some from the Wagon Wheel, some from the Frying Pan, all gleeful over the affair up in the Bad Country, all overflowing with what you might call camaraderie and, for cream on top of it, the milk of human kindness.

Babe Deveril leaped up and snagged Stet down out of his saddle after such fashion as caused Stet to go for his gun in a hurry. Then he saw who it was.

227

"You ol' son-a-gun," he cried joyously, and smote Deveril sledge-hammer fashion on the back. Then, his voice lowered: "Where's Miss Marian? How's she gettin' on?"

"How should I know where she is?" said Deveril, all innocence.

Stet Davis laughed him down.

"I asked Mother Mary," said Stet. "I says to Mother Mary, 'Where's Miss Marian gone to?' An' she looks me in the eye, and says, 'How do I know, Stet Davis, you good-for-nothin' scum of the earth?' An' I says back at her, 'Look here, Mother Mary,' I says. 'I want real bad to see that young lady.' An' then Mother Mary looks at me a while and she says, 'Hmf!' Know how she can say 'Hmf!' Babe? An' then she says, Mother Mary does, 'If you want to see Miss Marian, why you just go find Babe Deveril first! You watch where he goes, an' I bet you a pig pan of cookies against a wheat straw you won't be far from what you're lookin' for.' So let's have it, Babe."

Babe Deveril shook his head.

"Haven't seen her, so help me, Stet, since she left the Fryin' Pan." And then all of a sudden, watching the other punchers slide out of their saddles, throw their horses' reins over the hitching rail and start a stampede into the Long Horn bar, his inspiration smote him. It was an inspiration, like most of its breed, whose seed he himself had planted; planted when he talked to Mother Mary about Miss Marian giving music lessons!

"Stet! I got me a hunch as big and wide as a barn door. Listen!"

228

Stet listened. He seemed profoundly interested. He felt through his pockets.

"Hell, Babe," he said, "we ain't got that much money. I'm bettin' that all the boys in there, if you stood 'em on their heads and shook their pockets down, wouldn't shell out for ten bucks!"

"Let's go try 'em!" said Babe Deveril.

They allowed each man only one drink, then dragged them all over into a corner. They didn't do a lot of explaining to begin with. Stet Davis merely said:

"Boys, here's a great what-you-call human crisis. We need money. How much you boys got when we put it all together?"

They saw that he meant business and they emptied their pockets. Out of the crowd of them they raised about twenty-seven dollars, all spilled out onto the small green table. Stet Davis scooped it up.

"Come ahead," he invited. "Maybe you'll get another drink yet, maybe not."

They trooped out after him as he and Babe Deveril led the way to the Diamond Palace. Stet Davis stepped up to the roulette wheel, just started to spin. He plunked down his twenty-seven dollars on the red — and drew a deep breath.

Red came up.

Stet Davis said, "That gives us fifty-four bucks, gents! What'll we do? Let her ride or play the black?"

"Let 'er buck! Let 'er go! Stick on your same hoss, ol' kid. Red's good enough."

Though some voices said, "No, you damn fool, go on the black," Stet let it ride on the red.

Red came up.

"We got us one hundred and eight bucks, gents," he announced. "What'll we do?"

"Ten of 'em on the double-O," commanded Ches Mann.

"Five bucks on number nineteen — it's good, it's ripe, it's bearin' fruit!" yipped a voice from the rear.

Down went the two bets out of Stet's hand.

"One more hundred on the red —"

That voice was drowned out.

"Double the bet on the green, kid," said Babe Deveril.

Well, the double-O came up.

"We're off to a fine start —"

"We've just come to a fine stop," snorted Stet Davis. "This here money is for a purpose. How much we got anyhow?"

With a negligible few bets lost, they had about four hundred dollars.

Someone full of enthusiasm suggested: "Whoopee! Let's go!"

"Nothin' doin'," said Stet Davis magisterially. "Here, each one of you boys take five bucks; that's aplenty and it's more than you shelled out to begin with. Get half drunk, get something to eat, show up in the mornin' at ten o'clock, an' you'll get the rest of the story — Say, save out enough money to buy, each feller, either a harmonica or a accordeen, or something easy to play a tune on!"

The man who had suggested "Whoopee!" did so again, and they departed.

230

Babe Deveril kept discreetly in the background — and Marian Lee had a wonderful week.

It was a murky little window, scrubbed clean though it was. A cardboard sign, nicely lettered, announced: "MILLINERY: THE VERY NEWEST IN LADIES' HATS. PLEASE COME RIGHT IN!" And there was another sign, "MUSIC LESSONS HERE: VIOLIN, PIANO AND OTHER INSTRUMENTS."

A long, lean, lanky cowboy with an overlong wisp of straw-colored hair hanging down between his mild blue eyes, came to the door and cleared his throat and knocked, sort of timidly. It said, "Come in" under the hats; he was music-bent, and the music department had neglected to add the welcoming words.

He wiped his mouth organ on his chaps, properly took off his hat, and waited.

A voice, a truly lovely voice, called the omitted words: "Come in!"

Buck Willard, aged twenty-three, habitat the Wagon Wheel, stepped in on his tiptoes. His Adam's apple, very pronounced in a long throat, worked up and down.

"I was lookin' for the music teacher," he managed. He saw how pretty she was and, thought he didn't know why, he began slowly but inevitably to turn a turkey red. He gave his harmonica another swipe across his chaps. "I wanted to take lessons," he gulped.

Marian smiled. The poor boy, she thought, looked like a hopelessly lost sheep. She took immediate, motherly pity on him.

"On the harmonica?" she asked. She had tried to play a harmonica once or twice when she was a little girl in pigtails.

Buck brightened up.

"Yes'm," he said. "You see, I can already play pretty good. Only I can't read them dots with legs on 'em on music paper. Maybe you could show me? Here, here's how good I can play."

He played her "Turkey in the Straw" and her feet began to shuffle; she couldn't help it. He tried, "Oh Susanna!" and she wanted to sing it with him. He patted his foot while he played.

"Come back into my music room," she invited, very businesslike. She showed him the way through the calico-draped arch in the board partition. "And I — Oh, there's somebody at the door!"

Buck Willard, breathing deeply, stepping lightly, crouched through the door; a backward look showed him Busty James of the Two Bar-Q, hat in hand, entering the hat shop. Buck, hiding behind the curtain, watched and listened.

Busty twirled his hat. He, like Buck Williard before him, was taken a bit short-of-breath, seeing what the hat-shop woman looked like. Why didn't somebody tell him? He wondered whether she was married already? Shucks, no; too young. But not too young, judged Busty, to start thinking about getting married!

He had a little, young mustache; he twisted the short ends up.

"Howdy," he said, very polite. "Me, I come to buy a hat. Got one with blue ribbons onto it?"

It chanced that right in front of his nose was a wide, flap-brimmed straw hat very gay with the bluest of blue ribbons that ever were.

"Here's one —" the girl began.

"It's a dandy. I want that one," said Busty, and shoved out a handful of money. He remembered part of the speech he was to have made; he was buying a hat for his sister, for her birthday.

"I'll tell some of the other boys," said Busty, delighted with his purchase. "Lots of the time they likes to buy something for their — their sisters or — or their mamas; and what's nicer than a nice hat?"

He wore it amidst cheers at the Long Horn that night while doing an inspired tap dance, but Marian didn't know about that.

She gave Mr Buck Willard his lesson in reading dots on music paper, sold him the sheet music to boot, sent him away happy and two-thirds in melancholy love.

The day began well thus and rose into a crescendo. Every satisfied customer sent back another of his friends, perhaps a couple of them. She sold hats and she gave lessons on violin, mouth organ and accordion. Her little shop fairly rocked with music — or, at least, with good old-fashioned rangeland tunes.

That afternoon Marian Lee sat on a stool in her little denuded hat shop and sucked her knuckles. Her eyes were narrowed as though with suspicion, there was a pucker so deep between her brows as almost to be termed a scowl.

Mr Babe Deveril came sauntering in. He did not appear to have recognized her at first. Of course it was a place of dim light for one who had just stepped in from the brighter street. He began, head down, scuffling his toes:

"Lady, they've told me as maybe how I could get me a poke bonnet here. I'd be glad."

"A poke bonnet?" demanded Marian, and there was a glint in her eyes.

"Yes'm. You see, my gran-ma, she's got a birthday comin' up. An' I thought that maybe she'd like a poke bonnet powerful well."

"I am very sorry, sir, but I haven't any," said a precise Marian. "In fact I haven't a hat or a bonnet of any kind left!"

"I'm powerful sorry too," said the customer. He pulled an ancient harmonica out of his pocket. "Would you give me a music lesson?"

Not yet had he looked her straight in the face, not yet had he lifted his eyes from his scuffling boots. But now he did look straight ahead at the curtained doorway over which was the music room legend, and he stepped straightway through the curtain. The girl followed him.

Her violin lay on the table. He put his harmonica back into his pocket and took up her instrument. He ran the bow lightly across the strings. He didn't say a word to her — he played to her. He played with no master's touch, but warmly, humanly, musically; he played for her — to her — at her — an old, old song. It just happened to be one that she loved. She could almost hear the words as he laid the bow so softly across the strings:

"Oh, the heart that has truly loved never forgets,
　　But as truly loves on to the close,
As the sunflower turned to her god when he sets
　　The same face that she turned when he rose."

"Babe Deveril! I didn't know that you could play! *Like that!*"

He told her again about his ranch.

"I'm gettin' a team ready — four good horses to a light Studebaker wagon. We start in the mornin' early, with an outfit good enough to run us a couple of weeks anyhow. We camp out one night on the way, gettin' to our place the next afternoon —"

"*Our* place!'

"Sure. Suppose I want to stay bein' a hermit all my life? An' say —"

"Tell me about Temlock — about Crag Verilees! What happened?"

He rolled up his eyes.

"They've left for good," he told her.

"You don't mean —"

He nodded. "Yes. They — Well, they're not alive any more." He couldn't make the stern fact any softer than that!

"You — you killed them, Babe Deveril!"

He didn't answer; after all she hadn't even asked him a question. And she would learn in due time.

"Our wagon will be ready at daybreak," he said. "Want to go out an' take a look at our ranch, Marian? I'm totin' out just a little lumber; not enough for the whole house this load, but enough for the floor. Then we'll have us a dance. An' —"

"Babe Deveril! Haven't you *any* sense? Just because we — because we *had* to be alone a short time in the Bad Country — and you were wounded, too! — do you think I'll go traipsing all over the country alone with you?"

"Oh, I forgot to tell you: Charlie Sanders is workin' for us from now on. An', to celebrate, Mother Mary an' Johnny Sanders are comin' along. An' in a day or so there'll be a lot of the boys, bringin' girls with 'em, Stet Davis an' Ches Mann an' Buck Willard an' Busty Jim, an' bringing their girls —"

"And their mothers, all wearing their new hats with ribbons on them!" said Marian drily.

Babe Deveril had to grin.

"Oh, shucks, Marian! Sure they'll be along, an' most likely they'll be bringin' Parson Hibbons along too — Oh, girl! Will you come with me? I love you so — can't you somehow love me too?"

Well, he got his final answer a few evenings later when, just after the dance at Babe Deveril's new ranch, Parson Hibbons asked a simple question, and a happy, flushed Marian, stars in her eyes, her eyes shining on Babe Deveril, whispered:

"I do!"